Murder at Big Lake Resort

Written by Briannah Quick

ISBN: 979-8-218-51048-0

Chapter One

Staring at the clock Stacy Bernet could not believe that it was almost the beginning of the summer of 1985! She has spent the last eight months preparing for summer. After turning sixteen last month she knew her summer at Big Lake Resort was going to be amazing. Her family had been going to Big Lake since her father was a child and her grandparents before that. There were so many memories and one of Stacy's favorite places. With thirty minutes left on the clock she knew that this summer would be different. Her parents agreed to let Georgia Klusky, her best friend tag along for the beginning of the summer before Georgia's trip to Europe with her family. Stacy has already set up a job working at the resort's lifeguarding station while Georgia will be working at the information center. Sitting there all she could think about was being away from reality and spending as much time as possible out exploring. Stacy spent the last two weeks packing her favorite books, swimming suits, hiking gear and anything that she might need to have a summer full of excitement. Since her family went there every year she began to leave things at the cabin, like her bike that was too big and a pain to keep hauling around.

As the clock strikes three thirty and Stacy hears that final bell, she bolts out of the class keeping her eyes wandering for Georgia. Since both of them are sixteen their parents both agreed that Stacy could drive Georgia and herself to Big Lake Resort, as long as they followed Stacy's parents. As soon as Georgia and Stacy locked eyes Stacy blurted out;

"Are you ready for the most exciting summer of our teenage years?"

Georgia who was now in stride with Stacy replied *" You have no idea how excited I am to spend the first part of the summer away from my family, Claud has been driving me crazy."*

Claud was Georgia's brother who just turned thirteen, he was always asking questions and hoping that he could tag along.

The drive to Big Lake Resort was three hours from the small town of Milo. Georgia and Stacy are singing along to a cassette that was chosen out of a pile of both of their favorites. This included various forms of rock music from Stacy's pile and the hits from Georgia's. Even though they had a lot of similarities, they also had differences. With only an hour left of the drive they become more excited to see what this summer has in store for them. Georgia cannot keep quiet about the boys that they are going to meet. Asking Stacy all sorts of questions about what they are like. That is one thing that the girls don't have in common, Stacy would rather be alone and explore than to be trying to catch the attention of boys. However, this is the first time that Georgia's parents have allowed her to come stay at the cabin and they have been friends since first grade when Georgia moved here. Stacy plays along and answers Georgia's questions to the best of her knowledge.

Both girls start work Monday so they planned to spend the next two days unpacking, starting their summer tans and not having a care in the world. The information center won't have as much excitement as Stacy's lifeguarding job, but both girl's get off in early afternoon and plan to spend their time adventuring. Since Stacy has been coming here for the majority of her life, she knows of some great hiking trails and hidden waterfalls. Both Mr and Mrs. Bernet have allowed the girls total freedom since they will be busy watching Stacy's younger sister and enjoying time with their own friends whose families stay at Big Lake Resort too. Meaning other than working they wouldn't have many responsibilities.

Last summer Stacy noticed there was a new family that stayed in the cabin up the road from hers. Two boys and their parents occupied the cabin all summer. Her parents invited them over for a barbeque, they declined the offer but her mother did learn they were the Bock's from Richey. They were never outside much, at least not when her family was. One night she saw a tall blonde haired boy walking out of the house towards the dock. Stacy wasn't sure if he knew that she was watching or not but she was just curious of who he was. As soon as her family got home Stacy told Georgia about the family from Richey. Stacy hoped that this year the Bock's were more active and if not Georgia formed a plan to help break the boys out of their shells.

Driving past the large " **Welcome to Big Lake Resort**" sign, Stacy and Georgia let out a large loud shriek. Big Lake was a resort in the Crazy Mountains of Montana, there have been lots of stories about the fishing, wildlife experiences and beauty it brings. There have also been stories of people who have ended up going missing, Stacy has always thought, even though it's morbid, that the people who went missing didn't stay on trails, got stuck somewhere or have even been drug away by bears. She was not oblivious that nature made things happen either. In the hopes that it would never happen to her or anyone she knew, Stacy tried to stay on trails that her and her family were familiar with. However, she never gave up the chance to check out a new one if someone she knew told her about it.

"It's about time we arrive, the drive was fun but took forever" Georgia let out. Nodding with a big grin Stacy replied *"You know I have been looking forward to this month! There is so much to learn, plus working at the information center could give me an advantage to the history of Big Lake Resort!"*

"I know, I can't wait to show you all the types of insects that are crawling in the woods." Both girls let out a laugh.

Georgia knew that her job would not be as entertaining as Stacy's but she only had the responsibilities of handing out pamphlets, not making sure somebody's kid didn't drown. Pulling into the long driveway lined with large pine trees on both sides of the road they can feel the environment change. *"No more school or stress, just fun"* Stacy blurts out as the three story cabin comes into view putting her car into park. Georgia exits the car and starts grabbing her belongings to bring up to the third floor. The girls will have bedrooms right across the hallway from each other, which are the only two rooms on the third floor giving them privacy. *"Stacy, that is the smell of freedom and the start of an amazing summer!"*

Both girls spent the last hour getting all their stuff neatly put away and were sipping on a cold soda when they heard Mr. Bernet called for his wife. Walking down the stairs Stacy see's the tall blonde boy from last summer standing in the doorway with his family talking to her parents. The blonde boy and his brother look up at the girls who are now standing at the foot of the staircase.

" Don't be shy, you're never shy Stacy." Mr. Bernet says, giving her an eyebrow raised expression.

"Hi, I'm Stacy, this is Georgia. I remember you all from last summer!" Stacy gestures towards the family.

"Hi, I'm Claire Bock, my husband Brad, and these are my two sons Jonah and Bruce." pointing to a sandy blonde haired boy who needed a haircut first and then motioning towards the dark haired boy as she said Bruce.

"Are you staying all summer?" Stacy says with a smile.

"That is the plan, we really enjoyed it here last summer, we actually decided to buy the cabin up the street since it went on the market at the beginning of Spring." Brad leans more towards Mr. Bernet who looks like they are about to engage in a long boring conversation about the economy. Stacy let out a small snort, surprised both of her parents looking at her, and Stacy was not aware she did it out loud.

Chapter Two

After changing into their swimming suits, Stacy and Georgia head back downstairs. Neither of them knew how long the Bock's stayed and talked with her parents. Now that they are gone Stacy runs into the kitchen to let her parents know that they are going for a swim.

"Don't be too late, the Bock's invited us over for dinner." her mom says back.

"You mean the family we never saw outside last year wants us to come over for dinner?" Stacy's smart remark just came out.

"Yes, that is right Stacy. They seem like good people." Mrs. Bernet barks back. *"Now we are going over at seven, that gives you two hours to swim and be ready for dinner."*

"Yes ma'am." Stacy says back and her and Georgia are walking out the back door.

After the girls do a couple flips off the dock they lay their towels down to start tanning.

"Do you think it's weird that the Bock's all of a sudden came over?" Georgia asks while throwing on her tanning lotion.

"I know they declined my parents offer last summer to come out for a barbeque, but I think it's a little weird since we don't know anything about them and this is the first day here." Stacy says looking at Georgia who doesn't need tanning lotion. *"I'm kind of hoping it was just because they didn't know anyone and it was the first time we have seen them up here."*

" Let's just hope the boys aren't as boring as they looked, they didn't even say a word earlier." scoffs Georgia.

As seven o'clock starts to roll around the girls are walking back to the house and notice Bruce outside sitting at the dock. *" Should we go say hi or just wait until dinner? "* asks Stacy.

"I think we should wait until dinner, plus we have to change before my moms throws a fit." The girls throw a giggle and out of the corner of Stacy's eye she sees Bruce watching them. Running up the stairs, Stacy didn't realize that it was ten minutes until seven.

"You two better hurry, I told you not to be too long" Mrs. Bernet yells up the stairs.

As soon as the Bock's open the door Stacy's parents are smiling as if they have known this family for years. Stacy, Georgia and Halle (Stacy's younger sister) exchange looks and continue to walk in the house after the Bernet's. At first glance of the cabin you can tell it is pretty old, but the more you look at it you can see that some renovations have taken place. The smell of an old wood cabin is all too familiar, but it seems the Bock's have attempted to lay out fresheners.

Mr and Mrs Bernet brought a bottle of wine over that has been in the cellar for a long time. The Bock's decided that grilling was the best option to kick off the first dinner which means both groups of parents are chatting around the grill. Bruce and Jonah are sitting on the back patio furniture whispering to each other and Stacy and Georgia make their way towards them.

"Hey guys, how's it going?" Georgia is starring, waiting for a reply. After Bruce and Jonah exchange looks, Jonah pipes up *"Just talking about how the parents seem to be getting along really well."*

"Well hopefully they do or else the next three months would be awkward." Stacy chuckles.

"I'll second that." Bruce starts to laugh. Not too long later the parents are yelling that dinner is done and ask the boys to grab the refreshments from inside. Stacy thinks to herself that there is something mysterious about Bruce. He seems as if there is something that he is hiding and this person you are seeing in front of you is just a facade. While everyone is sitting down at the wood picnic table, Stacy makes sure to sit on the opposite side facing Bruce. She wants to know more about him but thinks that just observing is the best option right now. Scarfing down burgers and chips it seems the night is closing to an end. It wasn't shortly after that everyone said their goodbyes and Stacy's family walked back to their cabin.

Chapter Three

Laying in bed Stacy is having a hard time falling asleep. She walks over to her window that overlooks the dock and she see's Bruce sitting down there alone. Wondering what his fascination with the dock is, Stacy slips her shoes on and quietly walks downstairs and out the door.

"Hey." Stacy is walking up the dock closing the gap between Bruce and her.

"Hey." Bruce replies so quietly Stacy almost didn't hear him.

"What are you doing out here?"

"Just enjoying the water." Bruce looks over at her.

"You're not even in the water." Stacy returns his glance.

"You don't have to be in the water to enjoy it." Bruce looks off glancing over the lake that is still and barely

noticeable under the moonlight. *"There is something about the way the water looks so still, except for the bugs leaving little droplets of movement, plus the refreshening smell of lake trout."*

Stacy could agree with everything but the smell of trout, she enjoyed going out on fishing excursions but the smell reminded her of something that was rotting. Sitting on the dock in silence Stacy kept looking over at Bruce, she noticed the way his hair looked clean but not too clean, he was wearing shorts that might have just been old jeans cut off, and there was a fishing filet knife in his right pocket. After sitting there for what felt like a couple hours with seldom talking, Stacy and Bruce said their goodbyes again and went back to their own cabins.

The next morning Georgia is awakened by Stacy jumping on her bed. Georgia and Stacy are very similar except when it comes to their sleep schedules. Georgia likes to get as much sleep as she can while Stacy is an early bird and always wants to get a jump start on the day. Stacy tells Georgia to hurry up and get ready and she will meet her downstairs. By the time Georgia stumbles down the stairs Stacy is sitting at the island enjoying a cup of coffee.

"I started the coffee pot, cups are in the left cabinet above it. Do you want toast or are you feeling like a pastry?" Stacy lifts her mug to take a drink and glazes her eyes over to Georgia.

"I think I might have to settle for a pastry but I am going to toast it and have some fruit." Georgia, who just poured herself a cup of coffee, places it next to the empty chair next to Stacy.

"I have a hike I want to take you on! It leads to a pretty cool waterfall, however it takes a little while to get up there." Georgia now taking a seat, glances at the clock that sits above the stove reading five thirty.

"Since it's not even six yet I am glad you made coffee, I will be needing it." Georgia says as she stuffs her mouth with pineapple.

The girls finished their coffee and breakfast before six and thinking ahead, Stacy had already grabbed her hiking bag. Sorting out which snacks to take and grabbing extra water the girls are headed out the door.

"I had a hard time sleeping last night, so guess what?" Stacy, who is a little ahead of Georgia pipes up looking behind her.

"Um well, it must not have been a huge deal since you are chipper this morning." Georgia giggles knowing that

Stacy was going to tell her anyway. Stacy begins to tell Georgia about going down to the dock and sitting there with Bruce.

"So you're telling me that when I was getting some shut eye, you were out on the dock sitting next to the quiet neighbor boy!" Georgia exclaimed

Stacy laughs *"We didn't engage in much conversation, he is very quiet. More mysterious than anything."*

The girls are less than an hour into their hike when they decide to stop and rest for a couple minutes. Continuing their conversation and talking about random things, Stacy tells Georgia the hike is almost over as she peers down on the watch she keeps on her hiking bag. Georgia is glad to hear they have been walking for nearly three hours. The rush of the water starts to fill the girls' ears as they are rounding a corner. This is one of

Stacy's favorite places to be and where she will most likely spend any free time she has this summer.

"I was not expecting a waterfall this big!" Georgia glances over the scenery. Rushing down in front of her Georgia can see a nearly one hundred foot waterfall leading into a pool that flows to the creek. There are rocks large enough to jump off of too. Looking around, Georgia can see a space that allows someone to go behind the waterfall between the water and the flowers, Georgia agrees with Stacy. This is one of the most beautiful places she has ever encountered. Stacy wastes no time jumping into the water, Georgia follows shortly after.

"You never told me if you like Bruce." said Georgia and Stacy are now laying on towels working on their tans.

"That is because I don't know him. Talking to someone once doesn't help me decide if they are worth being liked. Like I told you earlier there is something off about him." Stacy says, flipping on her back.

"Are you going to spend more time with him?"

"I'm not sure, I guess if the occasion arises then I might. How about you? What do you think of Jonah?"

Stacy can feel a smile peeking from Georgia.

"Oh he's cute." the girls laugh. *"I might find myself spending some more time with Jonah as the summer progresses, maybe we can all take a trip up here?"*

Georgia longs to hear an answer of yes from Stacy.

"I think we can but do not be discouraged if they say no. Like I said, we did not see them outside a whole lot last summer, so they may not be the outdoor type."

Spending a majority of the day at the waterfall, it is nearly three in the afternoon when they decide to start the journey home. Arriving back at the house, Stacy was shocked that there was no movement. She walked to the back door and wouldn't you know it, there is her family and the Bock's enjoying some refreshments. They had pulled the horseshoes out from the shed and the cornhole boards were on the lawn. Stacy looked around but did not see any sign of the Bock boys. The girls make their way off the back patio and into the yard.

"Well there you two are!" Mrs Bernet says getting ready to pour more glasses of lemonade.

"I took Georgia to the waterfall!"

"How was it?" Stacy's father asks.

"As beautiful as ever, the water was warm enough to enjoy. I'm not sure Georgia enjoyed the hike up" Stacy looks over at Georgia who is beginning to chuckle.

"The hike was very long but it was worth it! Who knows we might end up doing it a couple more times!" Georgia exclaims.

After what seems like hours, the Bock's head home and Bernet's head to bed. Stacy wondered who the Bock boys were and what they may have been doing since they never showed up. She wondered if Bruce was going to end up back on the dock tonight. After reminiscing about the day, Stacy soon drifts off to sleep.

Chapter Four

Today is Monday, which means the girls start their first day of work! Stacy is already downstairs having breakfast and talking with her parents by the time Georgia rolls down the stairs.

"Good morning sleepy head! Are you ready for your first day of work?" Mr Bernet says as he grabs down a cup for Georgia.

"I am as ready as I'll ever be, plus it's kind of nice we don't have to be to work super early." Georgia takes the cup and pours herself some coffee.

"That is one positive thing, let's just hope the day goes smoothly." Stacy, now standing in front of the counter, checks the clock, *"We have to go to Georgia."*

The girls are walking out the door and at the end of the road they split ways. The information center is towards the entrance while the lifeguard station is a little farther down on the beach part of the lake. Already Stacy could feel a shift in the air as her summer truly began. In all the time she had been coming here, she now gets to see things from a different point of view. She gets to be the lifeguard sitting on the tall chair catching a tan instead of being the child whose parents won't let her go too deep in the water.

"See you soon, have a good first day!" Stacy yells at Georgia.

The lake so far is empty, which doesn't say much since it is only eight. In the next hour and a half there will be tons of children whose parents are nowhere to be found. Stacy remembers when she was younger she always had someone older with her. If it wasn't her parents, it was her grandparents. Sadly her grandparents had passed away a couple years ago, so now it is just her parents that bring her younger sister to the lake beach. As soon as Stacy gets to the guard shack her boss Susan tells her "hello". Stacy is ecstatic about being a part of this crew and she can barely hide her enthusiasm. Susan walks her through all the basic steps of clocking in/out, where to locate the first aid kits, and what items she should have in her fanny pack. It seems pretty simple, however Susan warns her that while there are not a lot of drownings, or people not being able to swim, the amount of people all at once can be overwhelming. She tells Stacy that no matter how she stays alert, bad things can happen in a split second. Stacy has known Susan for a couple of years, she taught her younger sister how to swim a while back. Stacy felt a relief when she got the lifeguarding job and heard that it was Susan who ran the shack.

The sun is beating down as it approaches noon. Susan was right, there are a lot of people which is a little bit overwhelming but Stacy is usually great in high pressure scenarios. Just like she imagined, there are not a ton of parents or guardians around, just lots of kids. The lake is open 24/7, but the beach part has curfews. This is to make sure that young children are out of harm's way when the sun starts going down. Since the curfew and closing time is at seven, they will have another lifeguard come on duty. A couple more hours and Stacy will be done for the day. She is looking forward to getting out of the sun because the small shade provided by the chair's umbrella doesn't go a long way! By quitting time the crowd has died down a little as parents tell their children they need to eat and drink something. Stacy reaches the time clock and is about to clock out when she notices a dark hair boy. As soon as he turns around she sees that it is Bruce. What are the odds that the boy next door, who only comes out at night is her co-worker?

"Well look at you saving lives." Stacy says to Bruce, who in return doesn't look very excited.

"I have to do something that keeps me out of trouble." Bruce replies without a single hint of emotion.

"Well, have a good shift." Stacy says as she walks out the door. What did he mean to keep him out of trouble? From the looks of it, the Bock's seem like every other family out there. Georgia is at the end of the road waiting for Stacy when she gets there.

The first words out of Georgia's mouth. *"Guess who I got to work with all day."* Stacy couldn't even answer before Georgia answered her own question. *"Jonah, he is very funny too."*

"That is a weird coincidence because Bruce is the night shift lifeguard."

Stacy wasn't sure how to feel about Bruce. Like always he didn't converse much. The girls are barely into the house before Stacy's parents are hounding them with questions about their first day at work. They were more excited than the girls, but Stacy thinks they are enjoying the quiet time to themselves. Besides Stacy's younger sister being there, her parents have a whole list of things they want to accomplish this summer. Her mother has plans of gardening and planting outdoor flowers while her dad plans to repaint the whole outside of the cabin, which is not a bad idea since it hasn't been done in over twenty years and it could use a new layer. For the most part the cabin has held together really well.

The Bernet family decided they wanted to take Stacy's younger sister to the beach, so they loaded up all of their toys and floaties. Georgia and Stacy joined them since Georgia did not want to partake in another hike this afternoon. As soon as they arrived at the beach Stacy's prediction was right, the beach got a lot busier after the children had eaten. Still like this morning, there was not a whole lot of parental supervision. Her parents chose a spot that had a little coverage from the trees, but close enough to lay out if they wanted to tan. Georgia spots Jonah coming towards them and hops up faster than you could snap your fingers.

"Hey Jonah!" The excitement in Georgia's voice made Stacy think she already had feelings for this stranger.

"Hey Georgia, hi everyone! Came out to enjoy the sun?

"We couldn't have asked for a more beautiful day. " Mrs Bernet says as she is lathering sunscreen on her youngest.

"Hey Georgia and Stacy, do you want to come hang out with me, maybe see if there is something cool we can do? " Jonah looks towards the girls awaiting approval.

"Just be safe. " Mr Bernet says.

With barely hearing her fathers words the girls and Jonah are already making their way towards the other side of the beach area. They pass Bruce on the way who is sitting in the lifeguard chair. Stacy can't help but notice he has no concern over the children, rather he looks like his parents made him get a job this summer.

"What's up bro? " Jonah and Bruce exchange looks.

"Just doing my civil duty, what are you all up to? "

"Just hanging out looking for something to do, you can join us when you get off work." Jonah looks to see if Bruce is taking the bait, he doesn't so the three of them continue on their walk.

"Have you guys noticed that older guy who just hangs around on the other side of the lake?" Jonah is questioning the girls. Stacy and Georgia look at each other and say almost in sync, *"no"*. Jonah continues to tell them he first saw him last summer when he was headed back from a hike late at night. Stacy wasn't sure if she ever noticed an older man in the woods when she went on her hikes. She has been coming here forever and her parents never warned her of a man lurking either.

The three of them end up joining a game of sand volleyball that lasted until the sun started to go down. The group of people they were playing with seemed to be a couple years older than the three of them. Stacy thought it was nice that the others didn't treat them like lousy kids. In fact the older group invited them to a bonfire this coming Saturday. As the night was coming to an end Stacy and Georgia said their goodbyes to Jonah and continued their way home. Georgia ranted the whole way about how great Jonah was and Stacy knew that if this is how it was already going knowing the guy for a week, the next month that Georgia was here was about to be really long. Mr and Mrs Bernet had dinner ready and were just sitting down as the girls walked into the house. *"We're in here."* Mr Bernet called out. After discussing how they spent their time at the beach area the girls told them about the bonfire. Stacy's parents agreed that it seemed like fun and a good way to make new friends. Catching up was how Mr and Mrs Bernet made sure they knew anything important going on in Stacy's life, and since Georgia was here with them they made sure to make her comfortable too. Georgia ranted to them just as she had done with Stacy, starting and ending the conversation with Jonah. The Bernet parents were more engaged in the conversation asking Georgia all types of questions, Stacy didn't get the impression that her parents thought it was anything more than a crush.

By the time everyone was in their rooms for the night, Stacy laid in bed wondering about the man in the woods. Her grandparents had never mentioned a lurker and it kinda caught Stacy by surprise. Throughout all the conversations tonight Stacy never brought it up. Getting out of bed she noticed the dock was empty. She put her shoes on and continued to make her way down the stairs and out the door. It was a quiet night, there wasn't a lot of movement across the lake. Stacy made sure to look in every direction of the treeline. She wasn't sure if she was attempting to prove Jonah wrong about the man or if she was trying to convince herself that there was someone out there watching. The more she thought about it, the creepier it got. After a while Stacy knew that if Bruce hadn't come to join her on the dock he was probably in for the night. Heading back to the house she heard movement, turning around as fast as she could. She sees him.

Chapter Five

A tall man appears out of the treeline on the other

shoreline of the lake, he looks ghostly. He is looking at

her, not saying one word. Just as he appeared Stacy

watched him disappear back into the woods. Stacy can

feel her heart start beating faster. Was she scared? Was it

curiosity? Stacy hurried back to the cabin.

After what seemed like only sleeping for an hour,

Stacey is awoken by Georgia jumping on her bed.

"Wake up dude! You're gonna be late for work!" At the

sound of Georgia's voice Stacy jolts up.

"You are very chipper this morning, what time is it?"

Stacy crawling out of bed asks.

"Well, you're not actually going to be late, I was just

surprised that I woke up before you did."

Continuing to chat and getting ready Stacy hopes that something will happen between Jonah and Georgia so she will stop talking about him. It hadn't even been a week since they arrived which means not even a week since Georgia met Jonah.

After their morning routine of hygiene, caffeine and breakfast the girls part ways at the end of the road heading to work. Stacy knows that when it's quitting time Georgia will share stories of the things Jonah did at work, she wasn't looking forward to that. She wanted time to think and just to listen to what was around her.

It had been raining the last couple hours, but the storm was clearing and it looked like it was going to bring in a clear and hot afternoon. Since no children were out swimming, Susan brought her some coffee to warm her up. Spending some time chatting and getting to know her. Stacy noticed that Susan must have grown up around Big Lake Resort. She told Stacy about another hike that she has never been on and encouraged her to check it out. As the storm begins to pass and the sun slowly starts to peak out behind the clouds, Stacy's shift comes to an end. Today was different, as Stacy was clocking out she didn't run into Bruce like she had every other day this week, and found it a little unusual. He is supposed to be at work before she leaves. Just as she has the last couple of days, Stacy and Georgia join each other on the walk home. Like Stacy predicted, Georgia is non stop talking about Jonah, however Stacy's head is elsewhere. The new hike she wanted to check out and the random guy that creeps around the woods, had her mind puzzled. She wondered if she sat on the dock again if he would appear. She wondered if Bruce really spent the night trying to lure whoever was in the woods out. Georgia finally stops the rant to see if Stacy heard her and asks what she should wear tonight.

"Tonight, what's tonight?"

"Did you not hear a word I said? Jonah wants to hang out tonight. I don't know what I should wear."

"I'm sorry, I must have missed that part. Maybe you should wear your orange shirt, you can wear whatever denim!"

Georgia gasps *"Why didn't I think about that!"*

Stacy turns and looks at Georgia, *"You can only think about Jonah right now so I doubt your brain will allow you to be the fashion police you truly are!"*

The girls approach the house and before Stacy has reached the steps, Georgia is already bolting up the stairs. Jonah is supposed to be coming by to pick her up in an hour, that means Stacy has enough time to change and go check out that new hike her boss was talking about. The nice thing about this hike is not as long as the one her and Georgia went on the day after they got to the Big Lake Resort. It would give her enough time to be back and in bed for another day of work. Tomorrow is Friday so Stacy will have officially made it through the first week of work. The bonfire is the next day!

Stacy tells everyone goodbye and lets her parents know that she will be back later. She gave her parents a little information on where she was going and informed them that Susan was the one who told her about this new spot. Instead of walking, she takes her bike that she had Mr. Bernet pull out of the shed yesterday and begins her trek down the road.

Closing in towards the end of a road Stacy see's a sign that says "*Dead End*" and from the description that Susan gave her she thinks she is in the right spot and if not she tells herself she will find out sooner than later. Placing the bike against a nearby tree, Stacy takes her hiking bag off the back and heads towards the treeline. Most places that have hiking trails usually have an informational plaque that stands next to the opening of the treeline to let hikers know the distance and if there are other trails along the way. Stacy doesn't see a sign and continues not thinking twice about spending a beautiful afternoon at a new place.

At first glance Stacy knows that others just think this is another neck of the woods. She notices which trees that birds have lived in or are planning on living in, the way the bark has been ripped off the trees shows animals that have antlers needed to itch their head or take the velvet off. Falling more in love with the woods each summer, Stacy has become so thankful that her grandparents grew up here but even more thankful they gave their house to her parents. She pictured herself living here after highschool. She wasn't even sure she wanted to go to college, so why not spend her life in a place that she adored? What if she became a mountain woman and created a life with animals just like Cinderella? Stacy felt the possibilities grow, life was full of unpredictable things and being out here was one challenge she always wanted to take on. She could learn to live off the Earth, she wasn't big into gardening but she knew if she had to she would make it happen. With the amount of wildlife that was around she would have a valuable source of protein, but she would have to learn to become a better hunter.

The air was crisp from the storm as Stacy followed an unknown path she could tell there hadn't a lot of human traffic. Susan was right, it was very beautiful. The trail itself was dainty, with small signs of the animals who have used it. She wondered when was the last time Susan herself came out here or how she learned about it. Stacy noted to herself to ask first thing in the next morning so she wouldn't forget. After walking up a huge hill Stacy could see the whole lake below, standing there she grabbed her water and took in her surroundings. She couldn't see any of the cabins surprisingly but was just high enough to see the lifeguard shack. It looked so small compared to when she was standing next to it. Given that the shack itself is old, it was a decent size. She remembers Susan telling her a short story of how it used to be someone's cabin. They lived there for many years but after they died their children didn't care for it and it was sold to a family friend of Susan's family in the early fifties. It baffled Stacy that someone wouldn't want a cabin that was right on the lake.

From what Susan told her there should be another waterfall somewhere up here that feeds the lake. The winters on Crazy Mountain can be insane, there are times when her family gets here at the beginning of June and the mountains are still snow capped. This year it seems the spring snowmelt happened early, she hasn't seen any sign of large runoffs happening. Stacy knew if she had gotten up here earlier in the year the possibility would grow. Continuing the trek Stacy doesn't remember Susan telling her about the terrain. Now she wishes she would have known. It wasn't that it was terrible, it was more uphill than the other hikes she was used to taking, leaving her to know that her legs would be sore in the morning. Walking what seemed to be another mile Stacy sees a small cabin further ahead.

As soon as she reaches the cabin she yells hello to see if there is anyone in it. Not hearing anything in return she pushes her way through the old door. The first thing she notices is the stench that smacks her in the face. The smell of a boys locker room, old wood and a musty lingering smell she cannot quite put her finger on. The cabin looks like it is lived in. There are pots in the sink, clothing draped over the end of an old couch. Stacy thought that no one could pay her to sit there. Helping herself to look around the rest of the house Stacy yells hello once again. Still nothing in return. Walking through

what seems to be the living room and down a hallway

she sees two rooms. The one on the left is a bathroom,

rust covers every inch of the tub,sink and toilet. Looking

around there isn't a toothbrush or soap of any kind.

Weird she thought to herself. She goes into the room at

the end of the hall. A bedroom. In the corner an old

mattress is laying on the floor, more dirty clothes are

skewed over the floor with an old pair of sneakers.

Curious to see if the water ran, Stacy goes back into the

bathroom. Turning each faucet on a couple small drips

comes out, then nothing. That makes sense for the pots

being stacked up in the kitchen. She goes back into the

kitchen, opens the fridge and a terrible smell goes

wafting out. Gagging as a deer head is staring back at her

and she hurries to close it, that was the smell. It's a musky smell of death.

That was enough for Stacy, she saw something new and notably something she never wanted to smell again. Was the guy who she saw the other night staying there? The man in the woods? Stacy didn't recall him looking as if he hadn't showered in a while, he just looked normal. Out of the house and back on the trail Stacy begins to hear water! The waterfall Susan told her about, finally! Rushing over, once again another hill in front of her she sees a thirty foot waterfall, and below it a large pool. What a beautiful sight, Stacy gasps filled with excitement. Good thing she wore a swimsuit because she cannot get the smell of the cabin out of her nose. Taking no hesitation she dives right into the water. At first it was a cold rush but swimming quickly takes the sting away. She climbs up on the ledge of the water and goes behind the waterfall. This is one of her favorite things to do. She runs her hands through the back of the water and feels the pressure dissipate into the pool. Magical moments like this are what she has come to love. Would she like to share it with someone? Yes, but here in this moment other than the few people she knew about, no one else knows about it. It was like a secret that she didn't want to share with anyone.

Chapter Six

With the air starting to cool off, Stacy decided that it was time to head back to the house. Putting all of her clothing back on and packing her hiking bag,she gets back to the trail. The hike was a lot easier going down than it was going up and she was thankful for that. Coming down the hill where that old cabin was, Stacy wondered if anyone was in there yet. She had spent almost two hours swimming and relaxing, it was a surprise she didn't lose track of time entirely. Looking around the outside of the cabin, Stacy peaks through the window that was at the side of the cabin. She doesn't see any movement or hear anything other than the animals outside. She thought about coming back to visit this cabin, only if there was a way to get that nasty smell out of there. This little cabin needs some restoration but it would make a beautiful place to live. Throw a little paint, new appliances, get the water running, this little run down cabin could be good as new. Maybe she can use some of the extra wood and supplies that her parents have, she would ask permission first but she doesn't think they would say no.

Stacy thought it was a good summer project, maybe when she worked up the courage to tell others she might include Georgia. Coming down a hill Stacy heard the crumbling of branches. Looking behind and around her, she didn't see anyone.

'Hello?" Stacy called out.

Her mind went wandering, was someone following her? How long has this person been out there? Was there someone in the cabin and saw her peering in the window? With no answer Stacy heard the sounds around her get louder. Still not seeing a human or an animal the noise seems right behind her. Not realizing how distracted she was by the noise Stacy is in a full on run. What if it was a bear, she shouldn't be running that would cause it to come after her. She slows her pace back to a fast walk. Closing in towards the end of the trail, Stacy can see her bike still against the tree. She turns to look around again, as soon as the sounds start they seem to stop just as abruptly. Climbing onto her bike she starts the journey back to her family's cabin. Stacy is barely pulling into the drive as Georgia comes running out of the house.

"It's about time you get back!"

"Well hello to you too." Stacy exclaims as she sets the bike against the shed.

"I have so much to tell you, Jonah is such a great person! I think we are very compatible." Georgia continued her rant but Stacy's mind was stuck on what was in the woods. Being out in the woods it wouldn't be out of the ordinary if it was an animal, and thinking that actually brings some ease to her mind.

The rest of the night was a blur, everyone sat down for dinner and dessert. Stacy engaged in conversations with her family but she wouldn't be able to recite anything if someone was to ask. A knock on the front door brings Stacy back to reality. It was almost nine, Mr and Mrs Bernet just went upstairs to put Stacy's younger sister to bed. Opening the front door Stacy's eyes widened at the sight of an old man. Not just a random man, the man she saw in the woods a few days back. He was scrawny with a white beard and looked as if he himself spent a lot of time in the woods.

"Hello." Stacy tried to hide the surprise in her voice.

"You need to be careful out there." The old man's voice was low and deep. How did he know where she was? Was he out there watching her? Was he the mysterious thing making the noise?

"Who are you?" Stacy lowers her voice, without an answer the man turned and walked down the driveway. Not looking back he disappears back into the trees. Stacy cannot believe what she just saw, let alone what she just heard. She stood with the door wide open, waiting for the man to look back or for something creepy to happen. Standing there for a few more moments, Stacy closed the door and went upstairs.

Chapter Seven

Stacy's eyes opened, not feeling rested at all, it was finally Friday. Stacy tossed around all night, she wasn't sure if she ever fell asleep or if she was in a trance of exhaustion. She has a list of questions for Susan when she gets to work, hoping that Susan would be able to answer them. She hears Georgia opening the door, she looks just as tired as Stacy.

"Do we have to go today?" Georgia motions for Stacy to make room on the bed.

"At least it's Friday, it's only the end of the first week." Stacy moves over, giving Georgia just enough room to lay down. The two girls decided that it was time to get up and proceed with their morning routines. Jonah is at the end of the driveway waiting for Georgia.

Arriving at work Stacy knows that it will be a busy day. Not only was it Friday but it was already almost eighty degrees and the sun was beating down. She tries to find Susan before heading to the guard shack but she is nowhere to be found. Stacy continues to grab everything she might need and makes sure that her lifeguard fanny pack is filled with the necessities to care for children and herself. Making her way down to the shack she notices Bruce is already there.

"What are you doing here?" Stacy finds Bruce rummaging through one of the drawers.

"Susan asked me to do a full day today since I missed yesterday."

"Ah, well I guess we can take turns rotating from the chair and being in here." Stacy looks over at Bruce. She hopes he picks up on the fact it wasn't a suggestion.

The summer heat has taken its toll on a bunch of families. Stacy recognizes some families that have been here before, others that might have come up for the day or are here for a weekend of tent camping. Usually she can tell who owns cabins by the way they talk to others and the ones who don't. Every year the beach area gets more populated but Stacy always feels a relief because she knows that they won't be moving in any time soon. The cabins that are around the Crazy Mountains don't go up for sale often, mostly because they are owned for generations but also because once someone moves in they seem to stay for a long time. The cabin that the Bock's bought last summer was the first one that was on the market in almost fifteen years. It makes it easy to get to know those around you, the people that spend their summer's up here seem like a tiny close knit community, unless they are like the Bock's and didn't have any interactions until this year. Mrs Bernet thinks it's because they were getting moved in, Stacy thinks in a sense that she might be right.

Getting out of her thoughts Bruce finally comes out to take Stacy's place, it's almost noon which means that the shack should be serving lunch. Sitting outside in the heat all day has made Stacy lose a lot of her appetite, so she chooses some fruit and water. By the time she is finished, she sees Susan walking up to the lifeguard shack, right away she bolts off taking towards her. Making sure Susan is able to answer her questions is very important to how Stacy continues with the cabin she saw yesterday. The first thing they discuss is history, Susan's grandparents' friends bought it and tried to keep it in their family. After years they decided that it was too much to keep up with during the spring as everyone had gotten older. Susan tells Stacy that the cabin went on the market a while ago but there were no bidders and after the last family didn't want it, it all went downhill. Stacy asks if she knows if there have been people living there. Susan assures her that it doesn't have the appropriate amenities. It would be hard to live there full time but it did not shock her if every now and then there were squatters who needed a place to stay, especially in the winter or when the rough thunderstorms hit.. During what must have felt more like an interrogation to Susan, Stacys asked what she thought about remodeling it. Susan agrees that it would make a great summer project, Stacy also shared the news about the dead deer head in the fridge. Susan and Stacy make a deal that if Stacy wanted to remodel it, Susan would help look for a cheap fridge to replace that one. Susan asked that Stacy keeps her updated with the renovations and asked her to invite her when she had it all done.

Stacy glanced over at the clock and realized it was quitting time. She had no idea that she spent so much time talking to Susan and thinking about the man who told her to be careful. She had so much excitement about the renovations that whatever warning the man gave her seemed to stop bothering her. Like she has everyday this week Stacy is walking towards her family's cabin and meets up with Georgia, however like this morning she is not alone. Jonah is next to her and they are talking and laughing. Stacy was glad that Georgia's plan about getting the boys out of their shell seemed to be working. She thought to herself, at least one of the boys was coming out of their shell. Catching up about their day and talking about the bonfire tomorrow night, the girls and Jonah split ways at the end of the driveway. Georgia questions Stacy about her hike yesterday and apologizes that she was so caught up in her date with Jonah she forgot to ask. Since Georgia was Stacy's best friend she decided that she couldn't hide the cabin from her. Georgia watched Stacy's voice change and get giddy as she told her about the cabin, the plans she has for the cabin and the beautiful waterfall. Just as Susan did, Georgia encourages her to make the renovations. Stacy wasn't sure that it would be done before Georgia had to leave but she promised to take lots of pictures and tell her about the progress during their phone calls.

When the girls arrived at the house they found Mr and Mrs Bernet firing up the grill. Stacy almost forgot that the first Friday of the summer her parents invite all the people over who knew her grandparents and they reminisce on the time they all enjoyed together. Stacy and Georgia head up the stairs to get ready. Stacy tries to warn Georgia about how the older community loves to get in your bubble. As much as she would hate it, Stacy reminds Georgia to be polite. It was around five when people started to show up, which gave everyone enough time to prepare themselves for questions that they might not have answers to. Mr Bernet was getting the grill ready, Stacy and Georgia were setting up places to sit, Mrs Bernet was handing out drinks to those that are arriving and Stacy's little sister was playing on the swingset her grandparents built for her dad when he was a child, surprisingly it is still standing. The weather has gotten the best of it but her dad made sure each time they come back that if someone were to use it, it wouldn't completely fall to the ground. Mrs Bernet always thought it was sweet of her husband to keep it in the family, but Stacy knew that at any moment it could be on its last leg.

By the time Mr Bernet had all the food grilled up and ready to serve, all the company had arrived and they were making rounds saying their hellos and how are you's. For the Bernet family that meant the questioning was about to begin and they began to brace themselves. It always starts with how school is, plans for the future, how was Mr Bernet's job going, simple questions before the hard ones. Stacy glances the yard looking for Georgia, when she finally spots her the Schullers have her backed into a corner. That poor girl Stacy thought, it was time for rescuing. Georgia's face fell with relief as she saw Stacy coming towards her. Stacy asked the Schullers if they had had a chance to get some of her mothers famous cherry pie, making it the perfect time for a get away.

"I tried to warn you, pretty overwhelming isn't it?"
Stacy and Georgia are walking towards the dock.

"I wish you would have told me that my whole life needed to be planned out by the time I was six." Georgia starts to laugh. *"Those people must know that life is a lot different than it was when they were our age, right?"*

" I honestly wished that I had an answer for you but sadly I don't. This happens every year and they ask the same questions. I think they hope each time that one of us crafted some genius invention or were movie stars. It is nice that my parents try to keep my grandparents' friends a part of our lives but there are only a few that

actually reach out to us after summer." Stacy and Georgia continue to rant and mimic some of the conversation they had when Georgia looks up, starts to yell and waves her hands excitedly. Stacy looks up and sees Bruce and Jonah making their way over to the dock. This is the time that Stacy knows that she will become a third wheel, well I guess both her and Bruce will be third wheeling. Besides work and that first night Stacy saw Bruce on the dock, they didn't talk much. It wasn't that Stacy didn't think he was interesting, it was more that he was so quiet Stacy wasn't sure what he even liked talking about.

Jonah and Georgia tell the other two they are going for a walk, leaving Bruce and Stacy sitting on the dock.

"Well I assume we won't see them for the rest of the night." Bruce quietly chuckles. *"I hope they know they aren't going to be getting married."*

Stacy who now is joining Bruce in laughter. *"I'm actually not sure they believe that, since they started hanging out, Jonah is all she likes to talk about, everything else is oblivious."*

"I guess that makes two of them, Jonah is starting to carry on conversation about her when he sleeps." Bruce starts laughing so hard, Stacy can't help but laugh when she hears a snort come from him.

Chapter Eight

The long evening is coming to an end as Stacy

crawls into her bed, she can tell she needs to drink more

water and apply more sunscreen because as her head hits

the pillow she feels the rush of pain. Bruce and Stacy sat

on the dock talking for a while and by the time they

called it a night, Georgia and Jonah were returning.

Georgia looks shocked to see the two of them sitting

there still engaged in a conversation. Stacy finds Bruce

quite the quipster, he doesn't try very hard to be funny he

was blessed with being witty. Stacy barely gets to think

about how excited she is about being able to sleep in

before she knocks out for the night.

The house is quiet, unusual since Stacy has a

younger sister who has yet to grasp the idea of sleeping

in but it's peaceful. Stacy climbs out of bed and goes to

Georgia's door. Opening it slightly, she sees Georgia is still asleep. Coming down the stairs she picks up a note from her parents saying they took her sister to the beach and will be back later. Stacy knows the bonfire is tonight but she wants to get a jump start on the cabin. She scarfs down some breakfast and goes to find what leftover materials she can in the shed.

It was shortly after that Georgia joined her. She had two different piles, one of things that were salvageable and the other that needed to go in the trash. Stacy of course would leave it for her parents to go through but it was things she would have thrown away a long time ago. Together Georgia and Stacy looked through the leftover paint colors and chose the one they thought would bring the cabin back to life. Since it was Saturday Georgia had made plans last night to go hang out with Jonah until the bonfire later that night, so she helped Stacy load the materials into her car and left. It was almost noon when Stacy was on her way to the deserted cabin, leaving a note for her parents and telling them she would see them later. She borrowed some tools she might need to do some of the repairs and headed out to start the innovations.

The drive was shorter than riding a bike, once Stacy arrived at the end of the road she forgot that the only way to get to the cabin was to walk. That meant many trips back and forth to carry all the supplies she had brought. Maybe Susan and her can come up with a driving path that she can drive her car on. She also did not want to ruin the woods but it would make things a lot easier in doing so. Three trips and lots of sweating Stacy has one last trip and she would have everything out of the car and to the cabin. The summer heat is starting to make Stacy think about taking a swim at the waterfall. She knew the first thing she needed to do was get the fridge out of the house, thankful that it's an older light model it was easy to move, but the stench did not leave. Stacy didn't think there was supposed to be a storm coming in tonight so she opened all the windows and hoped the refreshing air outside would help get the smell out. The last thing she wanted to do was start the repairs and painting so she put her hiking pack on and headed towards the waterfall. She knew that it was a little past three and she would still need to go back to the house and get ready for the bonfire but all she could think about was cooling off.

The rush of the water filled Stacy's ears as she came over the last hill. The water was glistening from the sunlight and in a matter of seconds Stacy was jumping in. She knew that once the cabin was finished she could enjoy life like this whenever she pleased. She might even work here during the winters if Susan and her could find the deed to the house. The possibilities of that could come from owning her own cabin brought more job to her life than anything she had done before. Including getting her drivers license. It was all about to become a fantasy life, one she had always dreamed of. It wouldn't be easy but Stacy knew that if she kept her nose to the grindstone it would get done faster. Making a mental list of other things to ask Susan she decided it was time to start her journey home.

The bonfire had more people than Stacy and Georgia thought would be there. They weren't even sure they saw this many people between both of their jobs.

Shortly after Jonah and Bruce make their way to the girls, they must have seen the surprised look on their faces because Jonah started to tell them a lot of the people are from the small town on the other side of the mountain. It was about an hour drive but it looked like most of them planned to stay the night because a line of tents were starting to form. Bruce asks the girls if they want a drink, both agree that it might help settle their nerves so they are left standing there as the two boys make their way towards the large group of people. Stacy was prepared to have an exhilarating summer, this year was full of beginnings and ones she couldn't wait to happen. When the boys arrived with the drinks the two girls cheered each other and began the mingling progress. Stacy talked to some really interesting people. Some were visiting family from other states, some stoners, drop outs, and others were musicians. They were a lot better than she thought and they ended up singing together around the fire. It was more cliche than she thought but she also wasn't sure what tonight would bring. Just as she imagined, Georgia and Jonah are talking. The way they carelessly talk to each other it would seem they have known one another for years. Stacy noticed the body language of her best friend, Georgia is sitting so close to Jonah and leaning in. Stacy wasn't sure if she was attempting to be kissed or see if he had boogers in his nose. Jonah, being a man, hasn't picked up on the hint.

Stacy continues to parade around meeting new people when she sees someone walking into the woods. Bruce. Where was he going by himself? Stacy, without thinking twice, started following in his footsteps, begging him to slow down so she could join him. Soon they are walking side by side through a patch of woods that Stacy was not familiar with. She made a mental note of coming here during sunlight because it was hard to see anything. Before they got too far into the woods Bruce suggested they head back to the party because the only light they have is from the bonfire and that had dimmed significantly.

Stacy did not partake in the drinking too much but she wouldn't say the same for Georgia. When Bruce and Stacy got back from the woods she left him to see how her best friend was doing. From what Stacy saw from yards away she knew not very well. Jonah was holding onto Georgia so she didn't fall over, it was very nice but Stacy could tell by the expression on his face he was ready to be done being used as a wall. Jonah helped

Stacy walk Georgia home and said goodbye as he headed back to the fire. Stacy tried to quietly get Georgia upstairs but it was not as quiet as she planned. Georgia was mumbling and her sentences did not make any sense, and Stacy barely got her to the bathroom before she started to throw up. It was going to be a long night. Stacy wasn't sure how much Georgia had to drink but she knew it was way too much to have her in this state. An hour and a half went by and Georgia's consciousness was back enough to let Stacy know she needed to go to bed. As any good person would do Stacy got her a puke bowl, placed some tylenol and water on the bed stand.

The night had been a great way to kick off the summer. Stacy met some cool people and she also found a new area to explore. She wasn't afraid of nature, but what that man said seemed to haunt her. For reasons unknown to her, she knew there had to be more to the story. What did that man know that he didn't want to share with anyone else? She had fun tonight, but as she lay in her bed the thought came rushing back to her. Stacy still hasn't told anyone about her random visitor or even seeing him that night in the woods. Turning to look at the clock Stacy couldn't believe that it was almost three in the morning. She wasn't sure what time she helped Georgia get into bed but she did not imagine that it was that late. Trying to clear her mind she needed to get some sleep, especially if she wanted to get a start on the cabin tomorrow.

Chapter Nine

Not having slept well, Stacy is awoken by the sounds of birds chirping. The house is quiet and she is sure that Georgia will be sleeping all day. Bouncing out of bed, Stacy throws new clothes on, places a little note on the table by the front door and grabs a couple snacks before she is out the door. Getting on her bike Stacy heads towards the cabin with only renovations on her mind. Arriving at the end of the road, Stacy places her bike against the tree like she has done a couple times before and prepares mentally for work that will need to be done in order to make the cabin livable.

Arriving at the cabin and stepping inside Stacy was glad she took the fridge out yesterday. The cabin was already losing its stench and she opened the windows to let some fresh air in. Stacy decided that she would start from the back of the house and leave the kitchen area for last, after putting on long gloves she started to move things out of the bedroom. Before she starts painting there is cleaning that needs to be done. She starts with cleaning out the windows, cutting the grime off with one of the razors she brought with her. She uses an old bucket she found under the kitchen sink to make a mixture of water and soap to clean the walls. She was happy that the cabin wasn't very tall so she could use a couple pieces of wood to reach the tops of the wall. It was a long overdue cleaning, after a couple of swipes her water was already turning brown. She couldn't imagine the last time someone had spent the time taking care of the cabin. The next thing to do is get the carpet out, she was glad that it was only in the bedroom. The carpet came up a lot easier than she thought, and it had a terrible smell to it. After placing the carpet outside Stacy thought to herself about how much time she would need to put into this cabin. It might take her all summer, she would do it after work and on the weekends but it was something she wanted to achieve before heading home.

The trim in the house was so old it was losing its color already and needed to be touched up so Stacy grabbed one of the cans of paint and started painting the trim. She wanted to keep all the walls the same color of white but she is not sure that there will be enough, so she choses a lavender purple to paint the bedroom, and leaves the white for the trim. The can of paint barely lasts enough to do one coat but it was way better than the previous color. The next part she wants to tackle is the bathroom. It needs to be rechalked around the sink and tub but there is a nice built-in shelf behind the door.

With no running water it makes it harder for Stacy to

clean but makes sure she adds it to the list of things she

needs to bring with her tomorrow. Stacy is proud of the

work that she has accomplished and has tried to stay on

top of leaving at a decent time but when she finished the

bathroom it was already dark. As she tidies up her

working things in the corner of the living room, Stacys

cracks the windows to allow it to continue to air out but

not enough that if it ended up raining that it would ruin

the inside of the house. Stepping out of the house she

hopes that she can find her way back to her bike, as she

wasn't as familiar with the trek in the dark. Besides the

small flashlight she has in her bag, Stacy is relying on

the moonlight to guide her.

Behind her she hears the crunching of sticks and leaf's, she assures herself that it was just an animal making their way around the woods. The noise kept getting closer to Stacy, she turned around to see if there was something behind her but every time she did, there was nothing. The only thing that came to mind was that old man telling her she needs to be careful out in the woods. The random warning filled her mind, not sure if it was a good idea to turn around. Stacy picked up her walking pace. The noise continued to follow her; she stepped behind a tree to see if it would vanish if whatever was there couldn't see her. With her back against a wide tree trunk, Stacy worked on slowing her breath down to become quieter. This worked until a deep voice made its way to her ears.

"Where are you hiding?"

Just as it slowed Stacy's heart rate began to fasten. Staying quiet and making sure not to move because the crunch from the woods floor would give away her hiding spot , Stacy began to think about how she could get to her bike, and fast. She didn't want to run directly into the woods knowing that she would most likely get lost, and she wasn't sure if she should get back on the trail when someone is obviously following her. Her mind went blank as the deep voice rang out again. *"I know you're there, why don't you come out and play."*

Once again not saying anything Stacy could feel the fear taking its toll on her, should she just stay put and when the sun starts to come up then make her get away? Maybe whoever is out there would give up and go back to wherever they came from. Whoever this person is, must have been the reason that the old man had warned her about being careful? What was she supposed to do, no go outside anymore? This summer, she couldn't just stay inside, she had work and family events. She had her best friend here to make memories with and enjoy the sun. The list of things Stacy wanted to do started flowing around her mind and she almost forgot she was hiding. She hadn't heard any noises or another sentence carried through the dark, so slowly Stacy started making her way back to the trail. When she finally finds it, she doesn't walk, she is in a full run clinging onto her backpack and hopefully putting some distance between her and whoever else is out there. She needs to get to her bike, whoever it is surely wouldn't follow her all the way home, would they? They wouldn't be able to keep up with her pedaling a bike and with them on foot, could they?

Stacy can see the end of the trail and her bike perched up against the tree. *"You're almost there"* she repeats to herself. Stepping off the trail she reaches her bike, with no hesitation Stacy gets on and starts pedaling as fast as she can. With what felt like forever, Stacy finally reaches the driveway to the family's cabin. Getting to the house she places her bike against the shed and goes through the backdoor. The house is still quiet and she wasn't sure what time it was. She lost track of time when she was doing the restorations on the cabin that she didn't even think about being home in time for dinner. Walking into the kitchen, she glances at the clock. It was almost midnight, she had spent over ten hours at the cabin. It sure did not feel like that Stacy thought to herself as she opened the cabinet for a glass. Pouring herself some water and waiting for her heart pace to become steady she walks over to the fridge to grab some leftovers. Her mother made her favorite pasta and ribs, without thinking to check to see if her parents were in bed Stacy warms the food up and heads upstairs to her room. By now if Georgia was home she would be sleeping or she might still be out with Jonah there was no telling when she would be back. Time was also not a strong suit for Georgia, that was why she always relied on Stacy.

Scarfing down her food, Stacy hops in the shower and gets ready for bed. Her mind is still wandering about who was out in the woods and if there was a connection with him and the other man who showed up at her house. Laying there she decided she needed a break from the cabin and that she should take someone with her the next time she goes. It would be better to have back up than to do what she did tonight again. She also needed a watch, she knew her dad was going into town the following day and made a note to ask him to pick her up a cheap one. Losing time was something she did not want to do again, especially not while she was at the cabin with a random person out there. With her mind still racing, Stacy slowly drifts asleep.

Chapter Ten

Starting the day out as she has the last couple work days, Stacy and Georgia are standing in the kitchen drinking coffee. Stacy had barely got her first sip down before Georgia started to ramble about Jonah. Stacy might have been looking at her but she was not retaining any information about what Georgia was saying. Her mind was still on that voice that carried through the woods talking to her. How long had they been out there? Were they watching Stacy the whole time she was at the cabin? She never thought to check outside if someone else was there, mostly because she was busy but because Susan said there was never a lot of traffic there. Stacy also knew this because the last couple times she has gone to the cabin or the waterfall she never saw anyone else. She only heard that voice last night, but never saw any indication that there was another human being out there. As she choked down the rest of her coffee, Stacy and Georgia took off.

Susan was already at work when Stacy arrived, it was not unusual but lately she had been coming in later in the mornings. Stacy clocked in, grabbed her lifeguard pack and was out the door after Susan.

"Hey Susan!"

"Good morning Stacy, are you ready for some beautiful weather?" Susan slowed her pace to allow Stacy to catch up.

"I am, however I had some questions I wanted to ask you." Stacy is looking at Susan, hinting that they stop walking.

"Sure, what's up?"

"So you know that I've been wandering around that cabin off the trail that you told me about. Well yesterday, I lost track of time and ended up leaving the cabin when it was already dark. But that's not the point. When I was walking back to the main road, there was someone following me. They spoke out into the woods a couple times, I did not speak back. I was just wondering if you know if someone else is out there? I haven't seen or heard any noise from anyone until last night."

Susan is staring at Stacy with big eyes. Stacy could tell with the look on her face Susan had left something out when they talked about the cabin last week.

"I am going to share with you something I already should have. There have been a couple summers up here where women have gone missing. They just vanish out of

nowhere and no one can find them. The park rangers try
their best to solve the mystery but the local police don't
want anything to do with it. If you are going to keep
going to the cabin alone, please be prepared for
anything. Make sure you leave when it's light outside and
if you get a weird feeling, always trust your gut."

What did Susan mean women have gone missing? Stacy and her family have been coming here her whole life and never was anyone warned about people going missing. Why would they not tell the public, especially since Stacy spends so much time out hiking by herself. Did that old man know something? Was it more than a warning? Stacy couldn't shake the idea that people have gone missing over the years, but before she knew it the beach area was starting to fill up and she needed to pay attention.

With the sun beating down, Susan came and offered to trade Stacy places so she could go for a quick swim. Stacy was happy to get in the water, she felt like she was starting to get heat stroke and she finished her water almost an hour ago. After a quick swim, Stacy headed over to the guard shack. Filling her water bottle up with ice water and reapplied sunscreen she peeked at the clock, it was only noon. She had a few more hours to go and thought she might spend a couple hours swimming. It is the middle of June, and once it gets closer to July the weather won't let anyone catch a break. It would start out with a nice morning, but by ten it would already be too hot. It was how every summer went, given the late night thunderstorms it was not about to cool down. One perk and downfall of being in the Crazy Mountains was the wind, some days it would blow really hard and other there was nothing. On days like this Stacy wanted the wind.

Climbing back into her lifeguard chair Stacy sees Bruce off in the distance headed to work. She had been so caught up in her mind she hadn't noticed him. She wasn't sure if he had been hanging out with Jonah and Georgia or just off doing his own thing. Bruce clocks in and comes towards the chair.

"How are things going?" Buce stares up at Stacy.

"It's way too hot to sit out here all day, but no one has drowned or started any fights." Stacy is quick to answer.

"What have you been up to? I haven't seen you since the fire."

"I tend to keep to myself, other than working I don't care too much about exploring the great outdoors. It's mostly

my parents' idea to come here, I would rather stay at

home." Bruce says.

"I don't see how you wouldn't want to explore. It's

fascinating up here." Stacy looks to see if Bruce's face

will gleam any curiosity.

"I guess if you think so you'll have to show me around

these "fascinating" places." Bruce says walking

towards the guard shack.

Stacy thought that might be a good idea, now that

she knew women have gone missing it wouldn't be such

a bad idea to have someone else with her at the cabin.

Stacy's shift is just about over and she heads to the shack

where Bruce is. He is talking with one of the cook's from

the grill when she walks in. Stacy and Bruce start small

talk but it quickly falls into Stacy telling him about the

trail and the cabin she is planning to live in one day.

Before they knew it, Bruce had agreed to go with her Saturday and even offered to help her bring up supplies. Stacy thought to herself that was a lot easier than she thought it was going to be. She for sure thought that Bruce would turn her down because it was too outdoorsy for him, Once again she was shocked. In hopes that her father got the note she left him on the table to grab her a watch and some more paint, Stacy would have enough supplies to finish the cabin.

The week went by fast as Stacy was finishing her Friday shift, she wanted to gather all the supplies and have them ready to be put in her car before Bruce and her head to the cabin in the morning. She told Bruce that the sooner they get out there the faster the work gets done and they can go to the waterfall, once again he obliged. This might be a good friendship, Stacy will be able to get Bruce out of his shell and she is rewarded by getting the cabin finished. Eating with Stacy's family, Georgia is talking about her plans for the next two weeks. Her family will be here in two weeks to get her so she wants to spend as much time with Jonah as possible. They have a couple different parties planned, some visits to the waterfall that Stacy brought her when they first got here and there was a new project that she wanted to finish at the information center before she left. Stacy was glad her friend was able to find happiness up here. When she invited her Georgia took some convincing but in the end here she was happier than she thought she would be.

Mr and Mrs Bernet made an easy grilled dinner but her mom also made upside down pineapple cake for dessert. Mrs Bernet was the baker of the family and her father did the cooking. It was a well balanced relationship, especially since Mrs Bernet did not know how to cook actual meals. Growing up Stacy saw her parents have the same relationship that her grandparents did, it was simple. Not much fighting and when Georgia would come over she always commented on how peaceful it was. Georgia's parents got along but there was always something that would happen and they would be fighting about it for weeks. Georgia tried to escape any time she could. Finishing the dessert Stacy's mother had prepared, the girls said their goodnights to Mr and Mrs Bernet and headed upstairs. Stacy hadn't told Georgia what happened the other night in the woods. She wasn't sure how she would react but knew that if she told Susan it would be best to tell Georgia as well. The girls sat in Georgia's room and Stacy went over everything that happened, even what Susan had told her.

"Why would you want to go back there?" Georgia's eyes were so wide with shock they Stacy thought they could have fallen out.

"It's like my own space, I get to decorate it however I want. It's like my own sanctuary with a waterfall less than a mile away from it."

After chatting a little bit more the girls decided it's time for bed. Georgia tells Stacy she wants to go to the cabin again before she leaves and will make sure it fits into her busy schedule. She tells her to be careful, she doesn't want her to go missing. Stacy thought that wasn't very reassuring but Georgia gave it a shot. Stacy lays in bed ready to get some sleep and mentally prepares herself to finish getting the old furniture out of the house and the kitchen painted. With an extra pair of

hands it will go faster and smoother than when she was

doing it by herself.

Chapter Eleven

By six o'clock Stacy and Bruce are in the car

headed to the cabin. When they arrive at the trail Bruce

blurts out that it is kinda sketchy. Just as Stacy had,

Bruce noticed the trail was not well taken care of. Stacy

tells him about the history of the trail and summarizes

everything that Susan had shared with her. Bruce said it

makes sense that not a lot of foot traffic has been around

here but Stacy warns him about the cabin. She hasn't

been to the cabin since Sunday and she'd hoped that

since the windows have been open for almost a week the

stench would be completely gone. The other things that

would have been holding the smell in is the old couch

and mattress but she moved the mattress out when she

repainted the bedroom. That just leaves the couch. She

notices Bruce sounds like he is having an asthma attack

as they continue down the trail. Stacy assumed he wasn't very active but she did not realize she should have touched up on her CPR. Yes, the trail is very long with up and down hills but she thought someone who is a lifeguard should at least have good lungs, unless he can't swim! Stacy chuckled to herself and before she knew it they had come up the hill to the cabin.

"Why would you want to do this? That trail is ridiculous!" Bruce gasping for air reached for his water. *"It might have been easier if we didn't have all these supplies, I promise the hike to the waterfall will feel like a breeze compared to that one."* Stacy can't help herself from laughing as she leads Bruce into the cabin.

The air smells a lot fresher and the paint in the bedroom and bathroom was now dry. It was time to tackle the worst parts, the living room and the kitchen.

Stacy and Bruce go over the plan to get everything outside, wash walls, counters, remove appliances and if they have time they will start painting. If not, Stacy told him she would come tomorrow and paint. She still had to find new appliances and hopefully figure out how to make a driveway. She doesn't mind the walk but there was no way she was able to carry a stove and fridge up all those hills. Catching a glimpse at her watch it was already almost three, she told Bruce thank you and if he wants to see the waterfall they should get going. Stacy enjoyed the company and she was glad they got their list finished. Without hesitation, Bruce was already out the door as soon as Stacy told him they could be done.

"No offense, but that place has a weird smell." Bruce blurted out as they headed to the falls.

"You have no idea! The first time I went in there a dead deer head was in the fridge, and you saw what the furniture looked like. It actually smells a lot better than it did, I'll have to find something to freshen it up after everything is done. Keeping the windows open has helped but I know even with scrubbing the walls and floors the stench might always be there." Stacy and Bruce continued to walk until the rush of water filled their ears.

"Oh thank goodness! I'm not sure I can walk anymore!" Bruce states and starts running and taking off this backpack at the same time as he sees the waterfall.

When Stacy gets to the edge of the pool, Bruce is already swimming and tells her to join. It was a really hot day, Stacy was glad she packed some extra water because usually three would be enough but was not today when there were two people drinking it. One of which seemed to be a fish.

For the next two hours Bruce and Stacy took turns swimmings, jumping off the rocks and laying out on the edge of the swim hole. Stacy was wrong about not wanting to share this place with someone else, it was exciting for her. She enjoyed showing others parts of the mountains she didn't know existed until earlier this summer and being able to have a secret waterfall. As Stacy sat on the rocks she looked around. Wondering if whoever was talking to her the other night in the woods, were out here watching her and Bruce. Susan said it had only seemed to women who have gone missing. Whoever it was taking them must be a man because usually women don't take other women. That is just a theory, Stacy could be wrong but she knew she was not taking any chances. She would be here when it was light outside and would tell someone who knew how to get here where she was. It was the safest plan she had because she didn't want to give up on the cabin.

As the sun began to go down Bruce and Stacy headed back down the trail towards the car. She had packed a few snacks but she needed real food in her system and by the way Bruce's stomach sounded in the car, she knew he needed a real meal too. Stacy pulled her car into the driveway and she could smell food on the grill. She offered Bruce to stay for dinner as a thank you for his help. Walking around the back of the house her father was manning the grill, her mother was sitting in a chair watching her younger sister play in the yard. Towards the house Stacy would see Georgia and Jonah engaged in conversation.

"Just can't seem to keep them apart." Bruce chuckles, nodding his head towards his brother.

"Well there you are, how is the cabin coming along? Did she overwork you Bruce?" Mr. Bernet pipes up as he closes the lid on the grill.

"I think she did most of the work, but I did think I was going to die on the hike up. I suppose it is a little harder on someone who doesn't know the terrain." Bruce takes a seat next to his brother.

"I'm glad that you said it, for a while there I thought I was going to have to perform CPR!" Stacy and Georgia laugh together. *"What did everyone do today?"* Stacy looks towards her mother to begin to tell her about her day and what adventures her younger sister had taken her mother on. Jonah and Georgia begin telling everyone what they had done and Mr. Bernet says it was time to

eat. Stacy was not only glad for the sappy love story to be over but was ready to stuff her face. Mrs. Bernet set the table earlier and just finished putting the side dishes on the table as everyone sat down. Each piece of food looked delicious and Stacy knew that after dinner there were not going to be any leftovers.

Chapter Twelve

Before the sun began to rise Stacy was already out of bed and headed towards the cabin on her bike. She didn't need to bring any new supplies today and it was absolutely gorgeous out. Arriving at the trail, it seemed to become a habit that she put her bike up against the tree and began her hike. Walking into the cabin the scent was almost gone, moving the old couch out was the best decision, if it had been done sooner she would have had this place almost smell free. Stacy grabbed her walkman from her backpack, put on one of her favorite tunes and got to work painting. The cabin was slowly coming together each day Stacy noted that adding an extra coat of paint to each room was needed. She barely had enough paint to finish the kitchen and living room. Stacy knew Mr. Bernet would be going to town again this following week and would add the paint to his list.

It was a hot day as the sun began to beat down through the trees, Stacy needed a break and went to the waterfall. She had left her watch at the house so she had no idea what time it was but knew the position of the sun meant it was late afternoon, maybe around four o'clock. By the time Stacy was ready to leave the sun began to come down. She was baffled at the fact she must have been at the waterfall for almost four hours, it never seemed that long. She got caught up in climbing the rocks to jump, walking behind the waterfall and taking in the nature that surrounded her. Stacy promised herself that she would always try to leave before dark and since she had left her backpack at the cabin she would have to make a stop there on the way to her bike. Grabbing her water bottle Stacy trekked back towards the cabin.

Instead of keeping an eye on the flowers near the path she caught herself looking out farther. The mountains can be deceiving, the way the tree's swarm around in the air and can go from barely able to move through into open spaces was always intriguing. When Stacy arrived at the cabin she did not grab her things right away. Instead she walked about outside looking for signs of an old driveway. There were small ruts that seemed to be the size of tire marks, but with the vegetation growing all these years, Stacy could not see where it went. There were clearing in the trees farther down but she was not sure if that was the actual road or if an animal needed to scratch its back. All of which could be an option up here. The bear population in the

Crazy Mountains was not small, she had seen a few tracks on the way up the trail last week. Stacy knew that just driving a vehicle up here would not be the best choice until she mapped out some type of road. Grabbing her bag from inside the cabin and doing a last minute walk through Stacy headed back down the trail.

Suddenly Stacy stopped as the sound of branches breaking filled her ears again. The sun was not down completely, it was still bright enough she did not need to use her flashlight. Looking around Stacy did not see anything. Her senses heightened and the hairs started to stand tall on her arms and the back of her neck. The movement got louder but still Stacy did not see anything. Attempting to calm her nerves, she convinced herself it was just an animal, clearly a heavier one. The leaves and branches that were scattered on the wood's floor did not make that much sound when she moved. Keeping her head up and turning around every few feet Stacy had a few hills to go and she would reach her bike. *Just stay calm, everything will be okay.*

"Well who do we have here?" a man's voice came out of nowhere and startled Stacy.

"Who are you?" Stacy demanded more than questioned. Waiting for a reply she continues to walk. Whoever it was knew she was here and alone. Stacy knew right then this man had been watching her. Her heart began to beat fast and the noise behind her got louder. She turned but once again did not see anyone. Stepping behind a huge tree, she sank to the ground and hugged her knees.

"Why are you always hiding from me?" the man's voice began to surround her.

Snap. Crunch. Break.

Stacy stayed quiet, she thought if she kept quiet like she did last time the man would go away and she could make a run for it.

"I like what you've done to the cabin. Got that terrible smell out." The man's voice is getting louder.

Staying put, Stacy tried to slow her breathing so it would be harder to hear her. Her mind is filled with thoughts. Was this the guy who took all the missing women? Was he a local? Where did he live? Stacy could feel her heart starting to race as the thought of her going missing began to raise panic. *Don't worry, you won't be one of those women.*

"You shouldn't be so scared, I'm just trying to make a new friend." The man let out a creepy chuckle.

Then there was silence. The eerie kind of silence, and as if all the hair on Stacy's body were not already standing up. She felt as if her heart was beating so loud everything in these woods would be able to find her.

"Boo, I found you!" a deep voice rang out from above her. One that Stacy thought she had heard before but was not sure where.

Stacy screamed, jumped up and began to run. A tall man with a heavy build came running after her. Branches breaking enclosed around her. Stacy's running came to an end and she tripped over a tree root. She fell forward and hit the ground. Scraping her palms and knees in the process.e began crawling and tried to get up as fast as she could. Scrambling to her feet, Stacy began to run forward again, found herself falling forward to the ground as something hard hit the back of her head.

"There. Now we can have a conversation without running." the man chuckled.

Stacy could feel herself being dragged across through branches as she began to gain consciousness. Her eyes barely opened as she peered up. The man held onto her ankles while walking face forward. He was wearing blue jeans, an old t-shirt and tennis shoes. Without knowing what she would do next, Stacy kicked as hard as she could. The man grunted as he fell to his knees as she turned to get away. She started off in a crawl and slowly made it to her feet checking behind her to make sure that he was still on the ground. He was now running full speed after her. Stacy started screaming for help as the man inched closer to her.

Smack.

Stacy began to cry not knowing what was going to happen or where this man was taking her. As the second blow to the back of her head hit, blood came rushing through her body. Then all her surroundings went black. The next time Stacy opened her eyes, she was not being ripped through the woods anymore. Instead she was sitting in a small one room cabin and a familiar scent filled her nose. The same smell that was in the cabin she had been restoring.

"Why are you doing this? Are you the man who took all those women?" Stacy said barely able to get the words out of her mouth without her head ringing in blinding pain.

"You know that's a good question, but you know the answer to that. Aren't you a bright little girl?" The man's voice arose behind her.

Stacy starts to cough and hears the rustling of bags behind her. The man walked around the stool Stacy is sitting on and looked at Stacy without any cover on his face. She sees a face she recognizes as he places a bottle

of water at her tied up feet.

"Bruce."

Chapter Thirteen

A vast grin emerges on the corners of Bruce's mouth. Staring blankly at Bruce, Stacy feels betrayed. Susan never said anything about the time frame of the woman going missing, but Bruce's family just started coming to *Big Lake Resort* last summer. How could no one see that something was off about him? How could she have not? Did his parents or Jonah know anything about his extracurricular activities?

"Why did you not say anything about the cabin, being you already knew about it?" Stacy barks. Her emotions began to get the best of her and she could feel herself getting angrier as Bruce stood there watching her.

"Some things are better left unsaid. That's what everyone says anyway." Bruce walked over to the kitchen.

Opening a drawer Bruce grabs a rusty kitchen knife. Tossing the knife hand to hand Bruce slowly starts speaking.

"You probably have a million questions. I will start you off, no one knows where this cabin is. My family brought my brother and I here one summer when I was ten. When I got my driver's license I would tell my family I was going camping with some friends. Instead I came here. I searched for an area that allowed a complete distraction from my other life. Something different, exciting, you know? Something thrilling. You're not the first person to question the why's. The "missing women" Bruce throws his hands up making air quotations. *"I chose them because they were always alone, much like you. Always out on their own, doing whatever they want, being*

oblivious to all the bad things that can happen to them

while doing such things."

Stacy stayed quiet listening and hanging on to each word that came out of Bruce's mouth. She could feel the saliva roll down her throat with every swallow. Her palms were sweating and she was not sure if it was blood dripping off the bottom of her hair or if it was a mixture of sweat and blood. It must be almost a hundred degrees in the little cabin.

"Don't look too concerned Stacy, we both know that someone will come looking for you. They won't be able to find you, but they can try." Bruce was now standing over Stacy with the knife still in his hands. *"So the more I looked around I finally found this area. I built a cabin over the last couple years, near a cave that a river flows next to. Meaning you can scream but only the birds can*

hear you. It wasn't something that I meant to happen with the first girl, it was an accident but I didn't want her to suffer. The couple after that became a habit, knowing that the woods are already dangerous, women like you think you can take on anything. Are you feeling like that now Stacy?"

Bruce sweeps the hair off her shoulder and touches it with the knife. Another large gulp drains down her throat.

"You do this for fun?" Stacy croaks.

"You don't think this is fun?" Bruce moving around her stops and looks down.

"No." Stacy replied in a stern but shaky voice.

"I had fun, I got to terrorize you and you still went back to the cabin alone. Did you think I was just gonna go away? I thought you had been warned, the old man

doesn't know how to keep his mouth shut, but I will deal
with him later."

Streams of tears are now running down Stacy's cheeks. She should have listened, she thought if it was still light outside it wouldn't have happened again. Bruce grabs a stool from the corner of the room and sits right in front of Stacy.

"You see, it's easy to have a hidden life up here, just like you wanted with restoring that cabin. You can easily get lost and have no idea how to find your way back. It's truly a simple thing to do. Large animals, cliffs, women go missing, families are devastated but each summer continue to come back. A true sad story." Stacy can hear the laughter being contained in his voice.

The knife is now making its way through the air and a rush of pain stings Stacy's leg. Stacy screeches in terror. Bruce pulls the knife out, gets out of the chair and heads towards the kitchen again. Stacy looks down, her thigh is filled with blood and it's dripping onto the floor. She can feel herself getting dizzy and lightheaded.

"Well I will tell you more when you wake up again."

Bruce walks past her and out the front door.

When Stacy wakes up she tries to move. It takes her a second to realize that her ankles and wrist are tied together with what seem to be rope. Stacy attempts to reach for the water bottle but it's too far away. It was now dark outside, her parents and Georgia would be expecting her home anytime now. Stacy has only shared a few things about the cabin with her parents, which means that they would have to rely on Georgia to help them get there. That was not the best idea, Georgia had never had any sense of direction. In the hopes that Bruce was still at the cabin with her she looked around. There was no sign of movement and she couldn't really see behind her so maybe he was asleep.

"Hello? Bruce, are you there?" Stacy's voice was still shaky. She needed to think of anything to take her mind off of the wound on her thigh.

With no response, Stacy tried to come up with a plan to get her hands and legs untied and make a run for it. If he wasn'here now, when would he be coming back? Stacy sitting on a small stool fell over and crawled her way into the kitchen area. Bracing herself up on her non wounded leg and the counter she tried using her mouth to open some drawers looking for something sharp that would help her. When she came across a drawer full of knife's, scalpels and scissors she stopped. Everything was clean. Were these the instruments Bruce has used on the other women? With her breathing getting heavier, Stacy used her teeth to grab one of the sharp items. Not knowing what she grabbed, Stacy let it drop to the floor. Her hands were tied behind her back and she needed to get her hands free before she could cut her feet free.

As she picked up what seemed to be a scalpel, Stacy was grunting from the intense pain of her head and leg. She did not understand what was amusing about this for Bruce. She recalls a previous conversation she had with him earlier this summer. She knew he kept to himself but she thought it was only because Georgia and herself were not a part of his friend group. Feeling the rope loosen around one of her wrists, Stacy tries to hurry to break her left one hand free. Just as her wrist slips out of the rope, Stacy hears a noise coming from outside.

"No, please no." Stacy quietly says. She needs to get her hands free and move back towards the stool. She could make him think that she fell off the stool when she lost consciousness or maybe it got uncomfortable sitting in that position. Sliding her way across the room. Stacy hears the front door creak stopping her halfway to the stool. The front door swings wide open as Bruce walks in with a lantern in full bloom.

"What do you think you're trying to do?" Bruce pushes the door closed and watches Stacy.

"Just needed to stretch out." Stacy knows Bruce can hear the fear in her voice, but what she doesn't understand is how calm he is. He moves around the kitchen acknowledging a drawer was open and closes it. Instead of trying to put Stacy back on the stool he leaves her in the middle of the floor.

"Now that you awake you should have some water."
Bruce casually walks forward opening the lid to the
water bottle he rested next to her feet earlier. Stacy knew
she had to pretend her hands were still tied together, if
not she wasn't sure what his next move would be.
Kneeling down next to Stacy, Bruce tilts the water to
give Stacy a drink. The first drop felt like heaven, or as
close to heaven she thought she could be in this
situation. This cabin was hot. The mixture of summer
and her openly bleeding leg Stacy couldn't get enough.
When Bruce tilted the bottle back, he looked shocked
she had just downed a full bottle. Stacy wasn't sure what
he expected when he stabbed her, hit her twice in the
head and left her tied up in a hot cabin.

*"Alright, now that we have taken care of that, where
were we?"* Bruce goes back to a drawer in the kitchen,

this time Stacy's back is facing him so she has no idea what he will come back with. The sounds of old metal clanking together is very unsettling. Stacy scoots her way more towards the wall so she has something to lean up against. As a few tears roll down her face, she strongly lays her wounded leg flat. Taking deeper breaths she turns to watch Bruce.

"You know, you could have just asked to be moved, it would have been a lot easier. I guess if that is where you are comfortable I will continue my story. Jonah and my parents have no idea about what I do when I'm not at the house or work. I keep them guessing just like you and your friend Georgia. A stupid girl for wanting to fall in love with someone who has a brother like me. She could end up missing too. Most of the search parties for the other woman only lasted seventy two hours. The local

police said they would keep their eyes open for any

suspicious activity but I take pride in hiding things. Plus

with the bear population everyone thinks those girls got

too close to cubs or a cave and attacks happened. But

you and I know that's not true." Bruce takes something

out of the draw and walks back to the living room.

"What do you mean hiding things?" Stacy gulps as the

words leave her lips.

"It's easy to get rid of clothes, shoes and bones. One

thing that is new for me is finding out what I am going to

do with your bike. You're the first person to have a bike

with them during my kidnapping escapades. Maybe I'll

take it down the mountain in the morning and some

stranger will grab it. You see Stacy, you're not going to

be found. Your belongings will be long gone before

someone notices that you haven't come home. Instead

you and I will be spending some quality time with one another. " Bruce picks up the lantern moving it towards Stacy. Her body is weak but she knows when the chance comes she needs to break free.

"You don't have to be afraid, I will end up killing you. You already know that though, there is no getting away from this Stacy. What a great friendship right? Short lived but we had some nice times. Like sitting on the dock, you looked like you wanted to have a conversation but as soon as I heard you were the adventure kind of gal all I could think of was ways to get you here. I knew you talked to Susan about the history of that cabin and when I watched you walk right into a death trap of repairing that cabin I wanted to join. To learn your mannerisms, I watched you from in the woods so I would know when

you planned on leaving. You never hid from me, it was me hiding from you." Bruce stops talking.

Sitting with only the glow from the lantern between them, Bruce is just watching her. No one is talking but somehow Stacy's mind is busy. Her thoughts and the actions that she can only imagine Bruce has done is setting in. *"I'm going to kill you"* is ringing like a siren in her mind. Stacy cannot believe what she is hearing. The lack of human tracks on the trail meant he found another route, leaving her and everyone else that they must have found their own safe haven. Now that's gone. The idea of her graduating school and moving into the cabin was completely wrecked but this psychopath, this murderer. She wondered if Bruce knew the other woman, or if it was just something out of pure evilness. A spur of the moment decision after the first *"accident"*.

Did he sit here, like this with them and give the same story? Stacy can feel herself getting lightheaded, she tries to shuffle her body more towards the wall and tries to keep her hands behind her back. If she lost consciousness again, she didn't want Bruce to know she had gotten one hand free so she tucks in underneath her. She attempts to take one large breath and her world turns dark again.

Chapter Fourteen

Bruce watches as Stacy's breathing gets weaker, he notices her leg has continued to bleed. Leaving a pool of blood on the floor. His other victim's didn't bleed that much when he had stabbed them in the leg, meaning that this time he had hit the artery. It was not supposed to happen like that. Bruce wanted her to stay around for at least a couple of days, so he grabbed an old rag and tried to slow the bleeding.

"What are you doing?" Stacy's weak and groggy voice comes out. As Stacy is opening her eyes she can feel pressure coming from her open wound. Bruce is kneeling beside her wrapping something around it.

"Ah come on, didn't think I would let you die that fast did you?"

Stacy noticed when Bruce speaks there is no humor. Instead his voice is stern with a hint of confusion. Why would he be confused? Stacy was under the impression that he had done this many times.

" Is there something wrong? I mean you said this is not your first time doing this. " Stacy shows no emotion, instead of being angry she is calm. Bruce told her of his plans and she has lost a lot of blood.

Coughing Stacy cannot hold her tongue. *"Bruce you're being weirdly quiet, I haven't heard you be this quiet since you kidnapped me. "*

Bruce was now sitting on the stool just watching Stacy as she winced. Stacy knew he was planning or thinking of the next way to torture her. Like something had bitten Bruce on the butt he was out of the stool walking towards the bathroom. There was no running water here just like the cabin Stacy wanted to live in. What was he doing?

Bruce walks back with a large tarp in his hands. Stacy noticed how dirty it was from the second the lantern's glow caught its form. She wasn't sure if it was dirt or a mixture of dirt and old blood. Her stomach began to become queasy and before she knew it Stacy was throwing up on Bruce's shoes.

"You could have warned a guy, I wouldn't have gotten that close." Bruce snared.

Something in Bruce's voice shifted, he was no longer confused but angry. In the matter of minutes his concern vanished. Stacy felt better after vomiting but she had a gut feeling something worse than being stabbed in the leg and told she was going to die was happening. Bruce popped open the tarp and a smell smacked Stacy in the face. Something she has never smelt before but imagined was the scent of decaying human flesh. Stacy gulped and her breathing began to stagger. She would have never pictured something like this would have happened to her. Not here, not at a place with so many happy memories of her family and of her grandparents. She had always wanted to be here, it was the only thing that kept her motivated during the spring. She knew that summer was coming soon and she got to be in her happy place. Well, what used to be her happy place, her family's happy place. That would be all over now, her parent's and younger sister would probably never come back here and **Big Lake Resort** would forever be known as the place their daughter and sister died.

Stacy's thinking is interrupted but the sound of Bruce clearing his throat. She looks up and sees Bruce.

His hands on both hips, smirking and staring right back at Stacy. It was as if Bruce was hinting for her to crawl onto the tarp, Stacy did not move. Even if she wanted to she would have to use her hands, one of which was free without Bruce's knowledge. Bruce walked around the tarp to the kitchen. Grabbing a variety of sharp instruments from the drawer Stacy found the scalpel. Neatly he laid them out on the counter assorting them from smallest to biggest. Stacy prepared herself to stab him if he got close to her, but she needed the right moment. One that would allow her enough time to cut her ankles free and get out the door. Bruce gathered the smallest bundle off the counter and carefully placed them in order on the tarp. Not one word was being spoken between the two. Stacy sat and watched the actions of Bruce as if he was the only one there. Bruce returned to the counter grabbing the larger bundle and did the same thing.

Looking over at the tarp Stacy saw a round fifteen items. The knives were the largest items and the scalpels the smallest, no scissors. Stacy was thankful for leaving the scissors out, she wasn't sure how he could have used them and she did not want to know. Bruce looks over at Stacy who is now more slumped against the wall. The rag that Bruce tied around her leg was soaked in blood, he thought the pressure was supposed to slow the bleeding, but Bruce was not a doctor. In fact, he was nothing more than a murderer in the eyes of Stacy. Walking around the tarp Bruce leans down and is inches away from Stacy's face.

"I made you a bed, shall we get you settled in?" The way Bruce spoke made the hairs on the back of Stacy's

neck stand up. It was still dark outside but she knew this would be her only chance to get away from Bruce.As Bruce began to wrap his arms around her torso, Stacy clings onto the scalpel that has been in her hand. When her weight begins to be lifted off the ground, Stacy takes her free hand and jams the scalpel into his back. Bruce winces and yells out in pain.

"What the hell!" Bruce drops Stacy towards the floor and runs to the bathroom to get the scalpel out of his back.

Without hesitation Stacy uses the wall to guide to get to her feet. Barely able to put weight on her wounded leg, Stacy tried her best to reach the door. Bruce is still in the bathroom when Stacy opens the door, she doesn't close it and tries her best to run. She knows that she needs to find somewhere to hide or get as far away as she can before Bruce sees that she is gone. With time to think Stacy is weaving her way through broken branches, she has no idea which way would be better and continues straight. She looks back towards the cabin, there is still no sign that Bruce knows she is gone yet. Not being able to see where she is going and only being guided by the little moonlight peeking out from the tops of the pines, Stacy continues straight.

"We both know you won't get far, Stacy." Bruce's voice comes crashing through her ears.

Stacy knows she can't stop, if she does he will find her but she as much as she hates that idea her leg is in too much pain to bear. Stacy stops using a tree trunk to hold her weight up, she needs rest but not with a psychopath coming after her. She should have grabbed the lantern so Bruce wouldn't have been able to use it but he would have seen the light and known exactly where she was. Pushing her weight off the tree Stacy continues moving. Stacy can feel herself getting weaker but she knows she cannot stop when she hears branches breaking behind her. Bruce was coming, and fast.

"Oh Stacy, come out wherever you are. A really clever thing you did back there, might have got you farther if I didn't stab the artery in your thigh." A loud laugh echoed through the trees.

Stacy can hear the humor come back into Bruce's voice. Was that what he was concerned about? How did he not know that was a possibility when you stab someone in the thigh! Stacy began to get angry, she needed to fight back. Whether it was fighting with her mind and body to keep running or Bruce himself she wasn't going to give up. Glancing back, Stacy could no longer see the cabin and as she turned forwards she smacked right into the chest of Bruce.

Bruce grabbed Stacy's body and attempted to hurl her over his back. As she was being thrown through the air, Stacy screamed and began to punch Bruce with the strength she had left. She could feel the dampness of his t-shirt where she had stabbed him. She punched one more time, hitting that same spot and Bruce gasped out in pain as he dropped her. She hurried to her feet and began to run as fast as she could. There was no telling how much time she had left before he found her again. It was not fast enough, Bruce came hurling towards her, tackling her to the ground making sure she did not get away again. Dragging her from behind the arms Stacy didn't stop her screaming. She continued to scream until she ran out of air.

"Why can't you just let me go?" Stacy's voice sounded like a stranger as the words left her body.

Bruce let out a large sigh, *"Why would I do that, I told you the plan, you are going to die. The quicker you come to terms with that, the easier this will be!"*

The door to the cabin was wide open, Bruce knew when he came out of the bathroom and the front door was open Stacy was gone. To Bruce it felt a little like a game, prey hunting for its dinner. The scenarios are almost similar, minus a few facts, but much like a bear chasing a deer Stacy would not get away. Bruce placed Stacy on the tarp, turning around and locking the door. Stacy looked over and grabbed a knife.

"Be careful, we wouldn't want you to hurt yourself." Bruce laughed walking around and Stacy had the knife pointed in the air following him. Why was Stacy fighting

this so much? Bruce's other victim never ran away, they never tried to hurt him either. Maybe Stacy was too smart for her own good, all she had done was make Bruce angrier. Stacy kept a steady watch on Bruce so he decided to sit down on the stool. Bruce knew soon her arm would get tired and he would make his move.

Stacy knew she would become weaker but she also knew the second that happened her fight would be over. She would have lost, it wasn't a fair fight but Stacy felt relief knowing that she at least tried. She knew her family would know that no matter what happens she tried. Stacy's arm gave out, waiting for Bruce to lurch at her she continued to watch him sitting on the stool. Angier and calmness in his eyes but his body language looked agitated. With no movement or talking, they both sat across one another watching, anticipating when someone was going to move. Stacy didn't want to pass out again, she knew that it was bound to happen with the amount of blood she had lost, the lack of having a meal or water would do her in. Stacy's body became heavy, like a weight sinking to the bottom of the ocean. She felt her body collapse onto the tarp beneath her.

Bruce watched as Stacy's body began to fold. When she hit the tarp, he sat on the stool for a moment longer. Making sure she nonconscious before making his next move towards her. Bruce wanted to be sure that there was no chance of being stabbed again. Bruce gathered up more rope from a bag in the living room and tied her legs and arms together. Once her arms and legs were together he tied the leftover rope to the table near her hands and the bottom of the fridge near her feet. Stacy was not getting away again. Making sure she was securely tied and the tarp completely under her Bruce

grabbed an item from the pile and began to make cuts

around Stacy's body. The more blood flow, the weaker

she would be when she wakes up, he knew if he hit

another artery she wouldn't wake up. Out of curiosity

Bruce wanted her to wake up, to see her reaction of

being completely vulnerable. After making several

incisions, Bruce walked over to where he was sitting in

the living room.

Chapter Fifteen

Bruce could see Stacy attempting to open her eyes, he had gotten worried because the sun had come up two hours ago. While he sat there watching her, he went over all the cuts he made. None of them were close to the main artery in her neck or arms. Just around them. Stacy's eyes opened, struggling to get her arms and feet free she laid there in defeat. This is what she didn't want to happen, she didn't mean to pass out again. Now it was too late. Glancing around the room, the sun was high enough to show the inside of the cabin. Bruce was sitting in a small lounge chair looking at her. He looked terrible, a lot different than Stacy would have ever imagined when he and his family had shown up for that barbecue. *"Glad you could join the land of the living one more time. I got a little worried for a second, thinking all my fun was over. You really pissed me off. Stabbing me in the back and then running off like that. It was stupid, but I got some of my frustration out while you were sleeping. Here you are, helpless but knowing what the future holds for you. Sad story isn't it?"* Bruce stands up and paces around the tarp.

"Now I won't be able to swim without a shirt for the rest of the summer, or people will start to ask questions. Questions are irrelevant, annoying and one thing I won't have any time for. All thanks to a dead girl. I hope you don't mind the extra restraints, I wasn't going to take my chances on you running out again. Ah, as you look around your body you will be able to see new cuts, it was very helpful in letting out my anger."

Stacy raises her head as far as she can and looks around her body. She felt new pain but thought she might have been delirious. Both arms were now covered in cuts, some shallow and others deep she could see the bone. Her chest felt heavy and light at the same time. From what she could see, one giant cut had been made down the middle of her chest. Blood flooded the tarp she was laying on. Bruce must have stepped in a pool of it because there were boot marks around the kitchen. Bruce kneeled beside her grabbing a scalpel.

"Don't worry, it will only hurt for a little while longer"

Pain wrenching from her stomach, Stacy started to scream. The scalpel cuts through layers of skin, penetrating towards her heart. Bruce pushes deeper, as his weight shifts Stacy can feel more pressure on her already open wounds.

"Please, stop." Her voice is so small and fragile. Her body barely had enough air to let the words out. Bruce

didn't stop, instead he cut deeper. The tip of the scalpel

is touching Stacy's heart. Stacy knew that was it. Bruce

would not listen to anything she said, she continued to

scream until the last gasp of air came out and the scalpel

stabbed her heart.

Bruce stood up over Stacy's lifeless body.

Covered in blood, Bruce walked out the front

door of the cabin. Grabbing the shovel from around the

corner, he paced into the woods. There were several

holes he needed to dig and knew it had to happen before

anyone noticed he wasn't home too. Scattered in

multiple places he would bury her clothing. Just because

someone finds a piece of clothing doesn't mean it would

belong to any of his victims. In all the searches

conducted for the missing women, not one article of

clothing had been found. Bruce intended to keep it that

way, and their bodies too. Being in this area of the woods, Bruce had never seen other humans which made it a lot easier. He would clean up the mess at the cabin, bury Stacy and her belongings then head back to his family's cabin. Act like nothing happened and he had no clue about anything, just as he had done before.

Arriving back to the cabin, Bruce stripped Stacy of her clothing and rolled her body up in the tarp. He picked her up carrying her out the door. The hole he had dug was about a mile away from the cabin, making sure that it was not close enough to bring issues if a bear found her. The hole was not your average six feet deep, instead Bruce has only dug around three feet deep. Throwing Stacy's rolled up body into the hole, Bruce started covering her with the dirt lying next to the hole. He finished burying her and headed back to grab her things. He placed her things into another hole, covered them up and left like he had done time and time before. He knew he needed to do something about the pools of blood all over the floor of the cabin, but without running water or towels it would have to wait. The other victims were far less messy and he didn't clean anything up.

It was still early morning as Bruce headed towards the resort. He made a pitstop to wash off in the waterfall that Stacy had brought him too just a couple days before. There needed to be no evidence so Bruce hopped in the water fully clothed. After giving himself and his clothes a bath, Bruce got out of the water and rung out his clothing before redressing. He knew that Stacy had rode her bike to the cabin so he would ride it back and place it in her family's yard before heading a couple cabins down to his own. If her bike was at the house everyone would think that she was upstairs sleeping, causing the search to be delayed. Bruce climbed onto Stacy's bike and began the journey back to the resort, what a simple plan and a dumb girl.

Arriving at the Bernet's residence, Bruce noticed all the lights were still off inside. It had to be almost six, which was good since it didn't seem this family were early birds. Placing Stacy's bike against the shed like he had seen her do a couple times before, Bruce headed down the road. Quietly entering the cabin Bruce headed to his room to shower and change clothes. The waterfall had helped but not as much as he wanted. Climbing into his own bed, Bruce closed his eyes to get a couple hours of sleep.

Chapter Sixteen

Two days ago, Georgia came down the stairs, she was just as shocked as everyone to know that Stacy was sleeping in. Georgia knew Stacy was never one to really sleep in, plus since she started the renovations on that cabin it was all she wanted to do. Georgia crept back up the stairs to see if Stacy was in her room. Opening the bedroom door to Stacy's room, Georgia noticed the bed was already made and no lights seemed to be on. She walked around the room, not finding any clues that Stacy was there. Georgia went back downstairs and told the Bernet's. They each had assumed that Stacy had headed to work already, but she usually made sure Georgia was awake. As the day went on the Bernets went about their day and Georgia walked to work with Jonah.

By mid afternoon and time to get off work Stacy wasn't waiting for Georgia to walk home. Georgia was enchanted with Jonah so at the time it wasn't something that was weird. Georgia knew that Stacy was probably at the house and getting ready to head to the cabin so she had made plans to hang out with Jonah for the rest of the evening. On the walk to the beach area Jonah and Georgia saw Bruce at the guard shack.

"Hey bro. How's it going?" Jonah spoke when he was in earshot of Bruce.

"Just doing my due diligence, watching over the kids." Bruce shifted his weight from one foot to the other. Jonah has no clue that his only brother was feared by multiple women. Georgia noticed that something was a little off today about him. He was always quiet and weird but something seemed to be bothering him. She wasn't

sure what it was so she kept quiet as Jonah and Bruce

continued small talk.

"Did you see Stacy when you got here?" Georgia asked

as she looked around to see if Stacy had jumped into the

water for a cool down.

" I can't say I did, I just clocked in and came out here."

Bruce acted as if he was looking around for her too.

"Well if you see her, let her know I'll be with you brother

please!" With that Jonah and Georgia continued their

way down the beach area.

By the time Georgia got back to the house it was

almost midnight. She knew that Stacy would already be

sleeping and she wasn't about to wake her up just to

share sappy love remarks. Georgia went up to her room

and got ready for bed. Knowing that in eight days her

parents would be here and she would have to go, Georgia

wanted her best friend to know everything about the things her and Jonah had talked about. The next morning ,Georgia turned over to look at the clock. She had to be at work in fifteen minutes! She hurried to get ready and was running out the door yelling goodbye at the Bernet's who were sitting down at the breakfast table. Georgia was angry Stacy did not wake her up! What had gotten into her? The whole time she had been here with the Bernet's, Stacy almost always woke her up for work but not these last two mornings. It began a ritual, Georgia got to sleep in and a too energized Stacy would wake her up. Running the whole way to work Georgia flew in the door out of breath.

"Easy killer." Jonah was laughing from behind the counter. He had just finished turning the lights on. Walking over Jonah handed Georgia a cup of coffee.

"I'm so sorry! I promise I won't be late again! Stacy didn't wake me up this morning, again!" Scrambling to find her breath Georgia was irritated. At least she wasn't too late.

" No worries, I was running a little behind this morning myself. Bruce had laundry in the dryer that wasn't dry so I had to find a pair of clothes that didn't make me look twelve. " Jonah and Georgia begin to laugh and go to work helping newcomers find their way around **Big Lake Resort**.

When the day draws to an end ,Jonah walks Georgia to the Bernet's cabin before heading back to his family's cabin. They have plans to meet after dinner to watch the sun go down. Georgia knew it was a fairytale she had been living in with Jonah but it was nice. He wasn't like the boys at their school. Neither Stacy or

Georgia could stand even being in the same classroom as some of them. When Georgia walked into the house it was quiet. The Bernet's must have taken Stacy's sister to the beach area.

"Stacy?" Georgia yelled from the bottom of the stairs. With no reply back, Georgia went to Stacy's room. Knocking on the door, she slowly opened it. Stacy's bed was still made, and nothing in the room had moved. The pile of dirty clothes by the bathroom didn't seem any bigger. *That's weird.* Georgia thought as she closed the door behind her and went to her room. Georgia had enough time before dinner she laid down to take a nap.

The sound of pots clanging together woke Georgia up. Getting out of bed, Georgia headed to the kitchen to see if Mrs. Bernet needed any help.

"Hi! Do you want help with anything?" Georgia grabbed

a glass of water and stood at the end of the counter.

"Well thank you for the offer but I think we are going to

keep dinner pretty simple tonight. Would you go see if

Stacy is here?"

Georgia knew that she wasn't home before her nap but

there was time for Stacy to slip in and take on herself or

work on another project. Coming back down the stairs,

Georgia looked in the backyard to see if Stacy was there.

"She's not in her room or out back." Georgia shouted

walking back towards the kitchen.

Mr and Mrs Bernet exchanged a look before looking at

Georgia.

"That's unusual. Have you seen her today, Georgia?"

Mrs. Bernet peers over the salad she is tossing.

"I'm afraid I haven't seen her the last two days."

"I will keep an eye out for her tonight and let her know this coming and going without any communication is not allowed." Mr. Bernet says sitting down ready for dinner.

After dinner was finished, Georgia helped clean up before Jonah came to get her. Telling the Bernet's not to wait up on her, Georgia and Jonah took off towards the sandy beach. The weather was gorgeous, watching the sun go down over the water had become one of Georgia's favorite things to do. About thirty minutes after the sun went down. Georgia told Jonah she didn't want to be late to work again the following morning. They packed up the blanket Jonah had brought to sit on and headed back towards the cabins.

"Stacy?' Mr. Bernet was sitting on the couch as Georgia walked in the door.

"No, sorry it's Georgia."

"Oh, how was your night? Did you see Stacy out there?"

"My night went really well, thank you. No sir, I didn't see her out there. She still hasn't come home?"

"Nope, no sign of her yet but you better get to bed. Goodnight Georgia."

"Goodnight Mr. Bernet, I'm sure she just lost track of time again." As the words left Georgia's mouth, she wasn't so sure anymore. Stacy promised her not to be out at the cabin after dark, if that's where she was. Setting an alarm and tucking herself in, Georgia wanted to wake Stacy up and ask her what had been going on. Georgia needed the best friend recap of events time.

The next morning Georgia had forgotten about the alarm she set and was startled awake. Taking her time to get ready, Georgia listened for any sign of movement from the house. Nothing, that meant everyone was still sleeping, including Stacy! Opening the door to Stacy's room, Georgia was shocked to see no one in the bed. It was still made and looked like someone had never slept in it. Walking down the stairs she glanced over into the living room. Mr. Bernet was asleep on the couch, in the same spot he had been sitting when she got home.

Coffee. Everyone would need coffee. Georgia went into the kitchen to start a pot of coffee, it was not shortly after the aroma had filled the air Mr. Bernet walked in to join her.

"Is Stacy upstairs? I must have fallen asleep waiting for her." Grabbing a coffee cup, Mr. Bernet looked at Georgia.

"I set an alarm because I wanted to wake her up today but she wasn't there. The bed was made, like it had been the last two mornings." Georgia had a softer tone, as the

words left her mouth her eyes searched Mr. Bernet's face. A loud ring cut through the silence.

"Hello?" Mr. Bernet's voice is still sleepy. *"Oh, hi Susan. How can I help you?"*

As Mr. Bernet waited to hear what Susan said, his face went cold.

"Sorry Susan, what do you mean Stacy hasn't been to work the last two days?"

Georgia looked towards the doorway as Mrs. Bernet was walking in. She had a look of concern on her face that matched her husbands.

"Okay, thank you Susan." Mr. Bernet hung the phone back on its hook and turned to his wife. He looked scared, unsure of where his daughter could be.

"Honey, Stacy never came home last night. That was

Susan, she said Stacy hasn't been to work the last two

days either."

Mrs. Bernet looked confused, how could they miss their

own daughter not coming home for days? What type of

parents did that? They told the girls they could have

freedom but that also meant being responsible. Trying to

calm his wife down, they all sat at the kitchen table

gripping their cups of coffee. After discussing what

should happen next, Mr. Bernet called the police.

Chapter Seventeen

The sound of police sirens filled the air. Unlike the rest of the summer, the early afternoon was rainy. The blue and red lights lit up the tree's in the small neighborhood. Mr and Mrs Benet called the police around eight A.M. Georgia sat at the table with Mrs. Bernet as the first knock came buzzing through the cabin.Stacy had not come back to the cabin in three days. Mr. Bernet found her bike at the shed and figured Stacy was upstairs sleeping but that thought soon came crashing down. The cops took statements from the Bernet's and Georgia. They each told them everything they could remember from the time they last saw her up until today. Mrs. Bernt was hysterical, but Georgia knew she had every right to be. After giving the police her statement, Georgia told them about the cabin Stacy had spent the last couple weeks renovating. When they asked for directions, Georgia could not remember. She had only been there once but told them to ask Susan because it used to belong to her family.

Mrs. Bernet asked Georgia to call her mother and let her know what had happened. It was too early to know anything but Georgia knew that her family would come. They would offer whatever comfort they could to the Bernet's. Georgia's parents would be coming in a few days to pick her up, it was only a matter of time before she would be on her way to Europe.

As the day was drawing to an end the police were still wandering in and out of the cabin. Georgia had not said one word since calling her parents and awaiting their arrival. She stood at the living room window, looking out but all she could see were neighbors watching. Still no Stacy. Georgia wondered what the families thought, how they would react to Stacy being gone. What measures would be taken to find her? By the late afternoon everyone around knew that Stacy had gone missing. Her bike, still perched on the shed, was unmoved. Georgia knew that if she was going to the cabin Stacy would have rode her bike or drove her car. Both are parked outside of the Bernet's cabin. Some looked shocked, while others must have known that something was going on in these woods. After the police had wandered through the neighborhood asking questions, some quiet remarks came back with the police.

Georgia's head was scrambling to find solace, something helpful that might help navigate the police's way to Stacy. The last person she knew that saw her was

Bruce a couple days prior. Stacy had mentioned that he was going to help her finish painting at the cabin. Georgia had thought nothing of it since she and Jonah had been spending so much time together she was secretly hoping Stacy and Bruce would do the same.

The storm had gotten heavier as a quiet knock came to the door. Mr and Mrs Bernet stayed sitting at the table engaged in conversation with one of the detectives. Georgia slowly moved from the window to see who was there as a cop opened the door. An old man was standing in the rain patiently waiting for the door to open.

"Hello, my name is Sam. I live in the woods over there." He turns to point past the dock and over the water. *" I came here tonight to offer some advice, maybe something that might help you find that missing girl."*

The policeman stood there offering the man to

come inside. Just as he walked through the doorway, Mr Bernet stood up,

"Sam, long time no see old friend."

"My apologies for the circumstances in which I am here. You know I like to keep to myself but your father was a friend of mine. It would be wrong for me not to come here and tell you what I know."

Mr. Bernet offered Sam a cup of coffee as he entered the kitchen. Sitting down next to Mrs. Bernet, Sam began talking.

"I saw your daughter wandering off into the woods a few weeks back. She left early in the morning and did not return until after dark. I had been waiting for her arrival so I could speak with her. When she had arrived home, I came over and knocked on the door. I told her to be careful out there. I am not sure why the warning of the

missing woman could not make its way out of my mouth, but I hoped she would not have taken my words lightly. It is not often I come out of my property to speak to others. There have been several women to go missing lately, no one seems to know anything other than the women liked to adventure in the woods. We both know it can be dangerous out there, not knowing what animal you might run into. I'm concerned that these women have gone missing, not by animals." Sam stops talking to take a drink of the coffee. Mrs. Bernet began to cry and excused herself from the table. Georgia remembered Stacy telling her about an old man who had paid her a visit. Stacy said she did not know who he was, but sitting there watching this old man talk, Georgia's heart sank even farther. Someone who had known Stacy's grandparents had warned her, he must have been looking out for her more than she knew.

Another knock at the door interrupted Georgia's thoughts. Watching her parents walk in the door, she got up and ran into her parents arms. Georgia had not shed one tear, but standing with her parents' arms wrapped warm around her she could not help herself. The police and the Bernet's filled Georgia's parents in on what was going on. They discussed a search party to start at eight the next morning. Georgia could not imagine sleeping, not with her best friend missing. She needed air and knew the dock was the only place where she would be comfortable. Putting her shoes on and notifying everyone in the house where she was going, Georgia walked out the front door.

Taking a seat on the dock, Georgia took her shoes off and placed her feet in the water. Tears began to run down her face, hating the fact she did not pay more attention. Georgia and Jonah had gotten so caught up in the moment, she rarely has stopped talking about him to see how Stacy was doing. She had only been to the cabin once with her and that was weeks ago. Now sitting on the dock, Georgia was unsure if she would ever see Stacy again.

Chapter Eighteen

As the sun began to rise, no one at the Bernet's cabin had gotten much sleep. The police left the residence a few hours ago and would be returning shortly to begin the search for Stacy. Georgia's mother began to make coffee and pastries for everyone. Her father was gathering water bottles, flashlights, poking sticks and bags to bring on the search. Mr and Mrs Bernet had not come out of their bedroom yet, Georgia was sure they were trying to prepare Stacy's younger sister before making an appearance. Georgia knew no matter what they said her life was going to be different. She was too young to fully understand what was going on or why there had been so many police at the cabin. Stacy's sister wouldn't know better than to think it was a game.

When the police arrived it was a quarter to eight. Mr and Mrs Bernet came out of the room to greet them. Mrs. Bernet informed the police that she would not be joining them in the search. Georgia's mother decided that she would stay at the house in order to help Mrs. Bernet with the young girl and anything else she might need done. The police agreed that might be the best option and gathered the ones who would be joining outside. Standing out on the lawn, the police informed Mr.Bernet that others were made aware of the search and had offered to join in. They stood there for a few minutes when multiple people began walking over towards the cabin. Almost the entire Bock family had showed up, Mrs. Bock stayed at the house in case Mrs. Bernet would be needing anything. Mr. Bock stood watching other familiar faces gather from the neighborhood. Fifteen minutes past eight, the police got a head count of everyone there and asked everyone to write their information down. In total twenty three people came to offer support.

The police informed everyone where the search was to start and where it would end today. Detective Raven, who was the head detective on this case, stood tall giving orders.

"There is a lot of woods out there, please make sure you are not walking alone and if there is any information found that you make it aware to one of the officers here. We have five officers joining us on this search and are hoping for the best outcome. Please stay patient with one another as we all want to find Stacy."

Georgia looked around, each face her eyes came across showed concern, except one. Bruce. His eyes were dark and cold. His body language seemed as if he had been drugged to join this search. Georgia's mind couldn't make sense of it, how could he not care? How could he seem indifferent? Jonah glanced at Georgia who was standing next to her father, with her best friend missing she almost forgot about Jonah. It was not that she didn't enjoy his company the last month they spent together but something much bigger was going on right now than a crush. Georgia offered a small wave and the crowd started down the road.

Arriving at the edge of the woods, Georgia noticed the familiarity of this area. The **"Dead End"** sign and trees were near the cabin Stacy had been working on. Georgia knew she had given such a great description of this area to the police, but Susan must have helped them more. Susan joined the search this morning, leading the police towards an area she grew up knowing well. Stopping ahead the police all turned around and detective Raven began to talk.

"This is where our search will begin, up ahead there is a cabin that we have been made aware Stacy was working on restoring. We ask that no one enters the cabin as we have a party already investigating it. There is a small trail that will lead you past the cabin towards a waterfall. Please keep your distance if you cannot swim. We are here today for work, not luxury. There are enough of us to divide into parties, but like stated earlier always have a partner to walk with. Many officers have already searched this area, but fresh eyes are always welcome. With that in mind, please be aware of where you are walking, and know where an officer is at all times. If there are any troubles, please notify one of the law

enforcement officers here and we will do our best to remedy the situation. We have mapped out a thirty mile radius, which would lead this search until dark. Please do not be afraid to go home at any time and know that we appreciate your help. Remember that we are looking for Stacy Bernet, any sign of trouble, injury, or belongings. Please do not touch any findings until you have gotten the police attention. We are going to allow the K-9 dogs to go first then after that everyone can follow suit."

Georgia took a deep breath as she and her father continued walking into the woods. Everyone soon began to disperse and the search officially began at nine A.M. walking close to the trail, Georgia could see the Bock family was ahead of her, her father and Mr. Bernet. As they got closer to the cabin Georgia's eyes wandered on

Bruce, he was smirking. It was as if Georgia was the only one to notice it. Stacy warned her of his weirdness before officially meeting him at the beginning of the summer but why did Georgia get the feeling that he was hiding something? Before arriving at the cabin, a group of officers were huddled around a tree. Whispering quietly to one another, detective Raven bent down taking a closer examination of the shrubbery. Georgia noted Bruce glancing towards detective Raven a few times, his face turned pale. Georgia knew at that moment, Bruce knew something that he was not telling the police.

Continuing their walk up the trail, officers stopped to take pictures. If there was any indication of Stacy here, Georgia thought the K-9 dogs would pick up her scent. She noticed they had not barked as much as she thought, indicating that her scent might have been washed away with yesterday's rain. Nearing the waterfall

that Stacy had shown Georgia a few weeks earlier,

Georgia began to cry again. Her father grabbed her hand

to offer remorse, but deep down she knew the pain of

Stacy missing might never go away. Walking around the

waterfall, Georgia noticed something shiny laying in the

grass. Getting her fathers attention, he and Mr. Bernet

stopped to watch her walk over to it. Calling an officer

over, Georgia watched as he picked up the object.

"Do you recognize this?" His gaze went from the

bracelet to Georgia's face.

 It was the friendship bracelet Georgia had given Stacy

when they were eight.

Holding up her wrist, Georgia pulled her sleeve up to

show the officer she was wearing the same one.

"That's Stacy's. I made them for us when we were little, we never took them off."

Mr. Bernet grabbed Georgia's shoulder, knowing this was hard for him too, she glanced up offering him a sly smile. *"It's going to be okay, we will find her."* As the words came out of her mouth, Georgia wasn't sure but it was something someone said in times like this.

Detective Raven told the officer to place the bracelet in an evidence bag and thanked Georgia for keeping her eyes open. Rounding the waterfall, tree's were the only thing Georgia could see. The trail had ended and they were now making their own. Officers had met with other searchers and each time there was an empty pit in Georgia's stomach. A feeling she never knew was possible, and she couldn't imagine her family being in this situation. Reaching for the map the officers had handed out, Georgia's father flashed the light on it. They were coming towards the end of the marked path. It had been dark for a few hours now and that meant everyone was supposed to head back. The officers marked a trail that would be faster for their return to the cabins and leaving a new area to search tomorrow.

Upon arriving back to the Bernet's cabin, Georgia's mother had prepared dinner for everyone in the search party. There was silence throughout the house and yard as everyone ate. It was not like the barbecue the Bernet's had hosted. The air was tense, full of remorse for the hurting, confusion to those who had been coming to **Big Lake Resort** for years. Georgia could not stand being near anyone. Hearing the low whispers of possible things that had been found in the woods today. Georgia could not eat so instead she walked down to the dock.

Taking a seat on the old wood, she gazed beyond the water. Somewhere in those woods was old man Sam, maybe he knew more or had seen more. He kept to himself but Georgia knew that did not mean he was not observant. The search began at eight again in the morning, and she was going to see Sam before then.

Chapter Nineteen

The sun was barely up as Georgia flew out the front door. She left a quick note next to the coffee pot explaining she went to visit Sam and would be back soon. Georgia knew it would be her mother who saw the note first and didn't want to cause worry to anyone at the cabin.

Climbing through some trees, Georgia saw a trail ahead, surely that had to lead to Sam's place. She continued to look for any evidence of Stacy until she reached an old cabin covered with trees and moss. Sam must not be one for renovations or upkeep. Walking up old wooden steps. Georgia noticed a swing on the porch. It was very homey. Knocking on the door, Sam looked puzzled to see Georgia standing at his doorway. *"Hello, my name is Georgia. Stacy is my best friend,"*

"Hello, it must be too early for a young girl like you to be out here. Would you like some coffee?"

"That would be great, thank you."

Walking into the cabin it looked as if Sam was married. Pictures covered the small table in the living room and the walls. It was clean, which did not make sense to Georgia as Sam looked like he was in need of a shave and bath. Grabbing a kettle off the stove, Sam turned on the water to fill it.

"Is there something that I can help you with?" Sam asks as he places the kettle on the burner.

"I apologize for it being so early in the morning. I was hoping you would be able to tell me more about the other women who have gone missing. If there were more connections made other than them being adventurous. If you have noticed any suspicious things or people around

that might help us locate where Stacy might be?"

Georgia watched Sam gather a few cups out of a cupboard and place them on the table. Sam looked at her before he beginning to speak,

"I am deeply sorry for the pain this has caused, Stacy going missing I mean. I have lived here for forty years, my wife passed away almost fifteen years ago. It was a lovely place to live. The first time we met was here at this lake, way before it had become a resort. There were more tree's and less than ten cabins. The Bernet's cabin was the closest one to us. A very lovely family. The cabin that Stacy had been restoring was a family home, but I am sure Susan has told you all about that. It was not until the past year and a half that weird things began to cause remorse over this beautiful place. It was early last spring when the word of a woman going missing came.

She was from out of state, out here on a hiking tour. She had wanted to see more before the group left. They were all camping down on the beach area. She ventured on her own one morning, and the next day her group grew concerned when she did not return. The police came and interviewed each of them. It was not the first time she had gone off by herself. They never found her or any of her belongings that she took with her. A couple months later, right before families started to come here for summer another young woman went missing." The sound of the kettle screaming stopped, as Sam poured coffee into both cups, then sat back down.

"*The second woman to go missing was no different than the first. She was also not from around here but instead of camping, she and a few friends were staying down the mountain in town. She reported her missing eight hours after she did not return to the hotel. Of course the police made them wait until the twenty four hour mark came. That should not be a rule, but the police do have jobs to do. After the second woman went missing, it seemed to quiet down around here. That was until late in August last summer. Everyone had packed up the week before, as school was to begin. Other than college students who were still enjoying the last week of vacation. A group of college students had come for the weekend, one of their friends had gone off before the sun arose and she never returned. The police got involved again but the search led nowhere. When I learned that Stacy was an adventurous person, I needed to warn her. The missing women were not much in the public view. Many people thought it was a bear but I know that is not true."*

Stunned by his last words Georgia took a sip of coffee.

"What do you mean, you know that's not true?"

Sam looked at her, placing his coffee on the table.

"My wife and I have never had any issues with the animals. In forty years, we have never had a bear attempt to attack us, even when there were cubs around. Whoever is doing this, is evil. There should be no such malice in someone, but it seems there is."

Georgia gulped as Sam's words crashed through her mind.

"You think someone is murdering women here?"

"It is very sad to say, but yes I do. I am truly sorry about Stacy, I hope there will be some news in today's search. I will be joining if that's okay." Sam picked up his coffee cup.

"Thank you, I assure you we would like all the help we can get."

After finishing their coffee, Sam and Georgia headed back to the Bernet's cabin. Georgia's mother was making breakfast as the two walked through the door. Greeting one another, Mr. Bernet was pleased Sam would be helping with the search. It was seven o'clock, the police had not yet arrived and everyone knew that shortly it would be time to go. The cabin was quiet, Georgia noticed the small talk was not enough to fill the void the Bernet's were feeling. Mrs. Bernet had barely said three words to anyone all morning and soon retired back to her bedroom. Georgia's mother told her Mrs. Bernet sat in the bath for hours while everyone was away yesterday. Mrs. Bernet had not eaten since the dinner two nights ago, and she only had a couple glasses of water.

Georgia could not imagine the pain that the Bernet's were feeling or what they may have to endure in the future. All she knew was she had to find out what happened to Stacy, and the other missing women. Even if it became the worst case scenario, Georgia was on a mission.

Chapter Twenty

Georgia noticed the search crews had become a little bigger this morning, even though she thought the whole resort was here yesterday. It seemed that word had gotten out in the town below the mountain and some locals decided to join. Detective Raven was the first to speak out loud as the search party had reached the new area.

By mid-afternoon, there was no sign of Stacy. Detective Raven notified a group of other investigators of a new area to search in the hopes that something would appear. While Georgia and her group continued to search the mapped out area, she couldn't help herself from wanting to get away from the others. She knew that with so many covering the mapped area, there wouldn't be the chance of missing something. The mapped area was only a small portion of the massive wooded area surrounding **Big Lake Resort**. The police only offered three days worth of searching, everyone in the Bernet cabin knew that would never be enough time.

Georgia knew that Stacy was not one to stay on trails and that her curiosity would have gotten the best of her if she wanted to explore more near the cabin. Trying to recall the last conversation Georgia and Stacy had, Georgia did not remember Stacy telling her about any other area that was not the waterfall and the cabin itself. The only person that would have known about future exploring would have been Bruce. Stacy came home late the night that her Bruce came to finish the cabin and they interacted with Stacy's family. No matter how hard Georgia tried to tell herself that Bruce didn't have anything to do with it, her gut couldn't shake the feeling that he did. Was she so blinded with Jonah that she didn't see the evil that could possess his brother? Sam was right, there was someone here that was murdering women and there was no telling if they lived here year round or nearby. After this catastrophe Georgia hoped that her parents would let her skip going to Europe, as the Bernet's would need help.

Towards the end of the mapped out area, detective Raven followed two investigators farther into the woods. There had not been a lot of commotion today, but something over there peaked their interest. Moving as far as she could to sneak a peek, Georgia slowly moved away from Mr. Bernet and her father. Peering into the woods, was a line of blood. The rain must have not reached that part of the woods because up until that spot there was only a few drops of blood to see. The grass was laid down as if something had been lying down for a while. As the investigators took samples of the blood, Georgia's eyes wandered around, there was a hillside that looked very challenging to climb up by yourself , let alone if you had hurt someone and carried them up. The only way that would have happened is if someone was being dragged behind them, which would exert a lot of energy. Whoever was murdering these women, had to be a man. Someone who was muscular and tall.

There were only a few people that came to Georgia's mind. Bruce, Mr. Bernet, and old man Sam. Quickly ruling out Mr. Bernet, Georgia knew he would not have been able to cause harm to his own daughter. He loved his family more than anything on this planet. Georgia did not know enough about Sam to completely rule him out of her own investigation. The talk they had this morning made Sam seem like a lonely widower. Not to mention how many years he had known the Bernet family. Bruce would be a project in itself. Georgia did not know a lot about who he was or what he did in his free time. Jonah spent little time talking about him or the things that interested his brother. Georgia knew it was a sibling thing, but the difference was that Jonah and Bruce were only a year apart, while Georgia and her brother had almost five years in between them. A list of terrible things that could have happened to Stacy cloud's Georgia's mind, the feeling in her gut makes it impossible to believe that Stacy is out here alive somewhere.

The sun was almost down when the search party was heading back to the residential area. It felt like another unsuccessful day, Georgia could see sadness and disappointment across Mr. Bernet's face. Knowing that it was not over, they would still have one more day of searching. Something was going to be found, and even if the police could not find anything, Georgia would.

Arriving back at the house, detective Raven informed the Bernet family that the blood samples found were sent off to the lab and the results would be back in the morning. Georgia knew this was good news, if the blood results came back to be human, that meant it had to be Stacy, right? Something that was that fresh and Stacy has been gone for three days. Detective Raven went over the plans on which area that would be conducting the search on tomorrow and told Mr. Bernet not to be alarmed when he heard loud sounds, because there would be a helicopter overhead assisting with the search. He informed everyone that after three days of searching with little evidence, it would not help the Chief's decision to continue. Detective Raven let them know that private searches are always welcome, and if any other evidence was found after the police were not involved to get a hold of him as soon as possible. After Mr. Bernet thanked Detective Raven, the house was quiet again. Georgia told her parents she would be back and left.

Chapter Twenty One

Walking down the road, Georgia headed to Sam's house. The more she knew about him the faster she would be able to cross him off her list of possible suspects Knocking on the door, Sam opened it looking just as shocked as he was this morning when Georiga came over.

"Hi, Sam. I hope it's alright that I came back here tonight."

"Georgia, you can come visit anytime you would like. It was nice having company this morning. I don't see much of my children so I will take all the visitors I can get."

Sitting down on the swing outside, Georgia waited for Sam to come back outside. Instead of making a list of questions to ask Sam, Georgia wanted to see what information he would offer her. If there was anything she wanted to talk more about it was the mysteriousness of people going missing lately. Knowing that Sam thought it was weird made Georgia more confident in her decisions about her list. If there was a chance to change her mind, tonight was the night. Georgia wanted to give Sam the benefit of the doubt but her friend was missing. Giving the benefit of the doubt to anyone was not going to be an easy thing to do.

Opening the door, Georgia got a whiff of something cooking in the kitchen. Whatever it was brought a familiar smell to Georgia's nostrils. Something that her mother would have made when she was a young child. Sam sat down next to Georgia in the swing, with a few moments of silence going by, he turned to her.

"I know that it's a very difficult time for you, and I hope that you do not mind me asking about Stacy."

Gulping down the air in her throat Georgia knew in that moment that Sam had nothing to do with her disappearance. Georgia felt relief come out and she began to tell Sam about her best friend.

"Stacy was always full of energy. There wasn't a day ever since we were children that she did not want to be out doing something. She always told me about Big Lake Resort growing up. Every year when the summer came to an end, she would come home the week before school started. The first thing we did and have always done was catch up on all our stories. Stacy's stories were a lot more adventurous and crazy than mine, but somehow when she would tell me about how her summer went I could always imagine myself here with her. I was so pleased when my family decided that I was old enough to

come with her this summer to see where Stacy had spent

all her summers."

Georgia could feel the swelling of the tears and knew that if she did not try to choke them back, they would fall. Instead she let them fall as Sam listened to the words she had to say.

"The two of you must have gotten along really well." Sam was offering Georgia some tissues.

"She was the closest thing I have to a sister, I have a little brother but it's not the same. I hope that whatever comes back from the lab tomorrow will help lead us in some direction. Stacy deserves that. The Bernet's deserve to know where she is or what may have happened to her."

Standing up and whisking his old body out of the swing, Sam looks at Georgia.

" Would you care to join me for dinner? I made homemade cornbread and chili."

"That sounds really tasty, thank you Sam."

Georgia had never tasted chili with so much flavor, the smell was like her mothers but with every bite she took her mouth watered for more. Something Georgia could never tell her mom, but it was one of the best meals she had ever had.

"You must really be enjoying that!" Sam let out a belly laugh,

"This chili is amazing Sam! Thank you for letting me stay."

"Your company is always welcome, everyone's is. People just choose to stay away because I'm a crazy looking man but in truth my wife always said I wouldn't harm a

fly. She was the more aggressive one and it only passed on to two of my children."

Laughing together and sharing the memories, Georgia was glad Sam was off of her list. Deep in her heart she knew he would be, but now she had to find out what truly happened to Stacy and whose hands were responsible.

Chapter Twenty Two

Everyone at the Bernet's cabin was silently waiting for detective Raven and his crew to show up. It was a quarter to eight, Georgia's mother made breakfast but barely anyone touched it. Mrs. Bernet had not come out of the bedroom this morning so her husband took her some coffee. It would most likely become cold and sit there before someone went and grabbed it .

Out of the corner of her eye, Georgia could see two cars pulling up the driveway. Detective Raven was here, hopefully with some good news. Mr. Bernet got up from the kitchen table and greeted him at the door. Detective Raven slowly walked into the house and asked Mrs.Bernet to come join them. Walking hastily to the bedroom, Mr. Bernet came out with his wife hand in hand.

"I think everyone here should take a seat." Detective Raven watched as several others sat around the kitchen table. *" You all know that while on our search yesterday several spots of blood had been found. You also know that what could be collected was sent off to the labs. Our office received the results this morning. The blood did not belong to an animal, which means the chief has given us his permission to continue to search that area and some of the surrounding areas that we can access on foot. The drops of blood came back as being less than a week old and human. If possible, Mr and Mrs Bernet, I would like to take some blood samples from you today in the chance that we find more on our searches. If this blood belongs to Stacy we would be able to use both of you for a DNA match."*

No time was wasted with the reaction of Mr and Mrs Bernet. They knew if there was a chance in finding their daughter they would do anything they could. Giving verbal confirmation to detective Raven, two of the men from his crew came over to get the samples.

"I do not want to scare anyone, but wherever Stacy is or whatever happened to her we will help you find as many answers as we can. With the expansion of the search, please be aware that it is also a dangerous area. The terrain is different from the other areas we have searched so I ask that only those who are capable and healthy enough to come along join us. As we have done everyday there will be a mapped out area, but fewer people. Meaning those to participate will have to cover more ground. We already have the helicopter out there searching overhead, if there is an area that is too

dangerous for us to get to he will let us know. Are there
any questions?"

Georgia's father had suffered from lower back
and knee problems her whole life, so he chose to stay
behind and help his wife. Leaving Mr. Bernet, Georgia,
and the Bock men to join. The others who had been
helping search were older so Mr. Bernet did not extend
the opportunity for their help this time. Instead it was
only the five that had gone and the men from detective
Raven's crew. Driving over to where everyone had left
off on the search yesterday, Georgia gets out of the truck.
Watching as Bruce, Jonah and Mr. Bock pulled in next to
them. Jonah greets everyone, giving Georgia a squeeze
on the shoulder. Georgia knew that if she needed to talk
Jonah would listen, but she felt herself leaning towards
Sam more. This situation they are all in would make

things and the feeling she had for Jonah this last month even more complicated, deep down they both knew that.

Walking over a hill, the view was amazing. Standing on the edge of the woods, Georgia had never seen a view so beautiful. The trees hung in just the right direction that offered the sunlight to peek through in various ways. Little areas were filled with light, while others were so dark the trunk of the tree's were almost invisible. It would be hard to find something in this area. Georgia knew that and accepted the challenge. She understood that no matter the cost, for her sanity and Stacy's family she had to do all she could.

The Bock's were ahead of Georgia and Mr. Bernet. Georgia watched as every move Bruce made was perfect. As if Bruce had been here before. The way Stacy described him being out of shape when she took him to the cabin was far from how he looked now. Making

smaller and larger steps than were necessary, and leading

his family to do the same. The police and detective

Raven made cautious steps before Bruce, but not as

detailed as he did. The curiosity of Georgia's mind

continued to grow, something was not right. Georgia

wondered if Mr. Bernet or Bruce's family members also

noticed how he moved with ease. Did detective Raven

glance back and see the particular motions Bruce made?

Maybe Georgia was over thinking, maybe she believed

that her friend's disappearance was at the hands of Bruce

too much. She did not have evidence proving anything

yet.

The terrain of this area created a firing sting in

Georgia's legs. She was not in shape for bouncing

around on mountain tops like Stacy was. Giving credit to

Stacy, a small laugh came from Georgia's mouth. Mr. Bernet looking at her, Georgia was just as surprised as he. There had been little talking on today's search, other than the police. The air was filled with tension, and the sound of puffing for air as everyone approached new hills. Out of the last three searches, Georgia felt in the pit of her stomach that this area was more than random woods. The blood drops persuaded detective Raven to go this way for a reason. One Georgia now knew.

Walking and leaning down next to a tree, a large amount of blood was resting on the tops of pine needles and grass. Georgia called detective Raven over to examine the area, in return he had his crew collect more samples. Watching as a police man cut various areas of the grass and gathered blood covered pine needles, Georgia noticed the top of the blood was dry but when it moved the inside remained a little wet. It was newer. Was Stacy out here?

After collecting the samples the search continued. Georgia watched Bruce's facial expressions as the police conversed about the blood droplets. Going from a normal shade to almost pale. If it was not for Georgia believing Bruce had something to do with Stacy's disappearance, his reaction might have just been that bodily fluids make him queasy. Georgia did not buy it.

Bruce pretended not to know where he was, which was hard to do. He had scaled this area on many occasions. The other police searches never extended this far, which created a small amount of panic in his stomach. It was only a few days ago that he drugged Stacy up this hill and ran after her. He consciously made the decisions of going ahead of his brother and father. Walking behind the police crew he could act as if their path was too dangerous and could help his family navigate better. His palms began to sweat as they got closer to the cabin. Around the corner of this hill was an entry point to his secrets. He needed to prevent that and immediately looked for a "safer" route for everyone to go.

Mr. Bernet and Georgia went ahead of the Bock's going over another hillside, it was steep and the passage below was full of rocks. Each step was taken seriously as everyone followed the person in front of them in a formal line. Georgia noticed the path ahead broke towards the left, giving them the options.

Chapter Twenty Three

"Hey let's look this way over," Bruce called from behind pointing towards the left of the path they were on. He knew that if the search party continued on, it would lead them to the large rock that barely covered the hidden cabin. The cabin that held all of his secrets. Where all his victims took their last breath and where his blood would be on several things from where Stacy stabbed him. His shoulder was still in pain, but he knew if he talked about it, the police would question him. Something he did not want and needed to prevent. He would get caught, and everyone would know that he killed Stacy and the other woman.

The placement of the cabin would have not been recognizable in the helicopter. It would have looked like another earthly formation. Bruce had all intentions to keep it that way. He had not been back to the cabin since he buried Stacy and her belongings. The only way Bruce would have been able to do any cleaning would have to wait until they stop the searching all together. The blood samples that keep appearing would make that difficult. He had hoped the rain washed away any evidence of Stacy. He was wrong. The thought of anyone finding out that he had something to do with her disappearance made his stomach drop. No one was ever supposed to know. It was a secret he wanted to continue hiding.

Georgia turned around just in time to see Bruce in mid thought. What was he hiding ahead? Why did the police listen to him? She made a cautious decision that even if she came alone, she would go see what was ahead. The search was coming to an end as the sun began to fate along the tree line. Depending on what the lab says about the blood, would depend on where detective Raven mapped for the next search. Georgia knew it could only be a matter of time before they called the search off.

Walking into the front door of the Bernet's cabin, the smell of dinner was seeping from the kitchen. Mr. Bernet offered the police crew to stay and everyone piled into the kitchen.

"Thank you for letting us stay, I know this is a difficult time for you all. Please know with the amount of evidence collected today it might take longer to get the results from the lab. I am hopeful that we will have them tomorrow evening. You have the option to continue to search tomorrow or take the day off and we can wait for the results. " Detective Raven spoke with such clearness, as if he was hoping for a day off from hiking.

Standing up, Mr. Bernet shook detective Raven's hand. *"I fully understand and believe that a day off will help everyone recover. As soon as you know, please reach out."*

A day. That was all Georgia needed. She could leave early in the morning and make sure that no one, not even Bruce was awake to see her go. From where they ended the search today, gave her a faster walkway to the area Bruce suggested we not go. Thinking about the things she would need, Georgia scarfed down the dinner her parents had prepared and told everyone she was off to bed. Going to the dresser, Georgia opened a drawer and retrieved the polaroid camera. If there was anything to find, having pictures as proof would help.

Grabbing the bag she had been using for the searches, Georgia emptied it out. Repacking the essential things and adding a few more. When the house was quiet she snuck downstairs to grab small baggies from the kitchen. Opening and closing drawers as mouse-like as she could, Georgia knew there had to be some type of rubber gloves. After finding what she needed, she wrote a quick note for her parents and prepared herself for a couple hours of sleep.

Chapter Twenty Four

The sun was still sleeping as Georgia climbed out of her bed. Stepping as softly as she could, she snuck out the door into the early morning dew. Knowing a vehicle would make too much noise,Georgia decided to take Mrs. Bernet's bike. There was no way she would be able to ride Stacy's. It hadn't been moved and she was not about to move it. Pedaling off into the darkness, Georgia couldn't think about anything than the way Bruce acted yesterday.

Placing Mrs. Bernet's bike against a tree, the calming sounds of the birds chirping filled Georgia's ears. The sun had begun to shine slightly through the trees giving Georgia enough light she did not need her flashlight anymore. Moving as careful as she did the day before Georgia approached the hillside where Bruce made them veer left. Feeling her heart begin to race, it was the moment of truth. Following a very well hidden path of trees Georgia came to a large rock. A rock? That was what Bruce did not want anyone to see? She knew that couldn't be the truth, there was something more. What was she missing? Being careful to take in her surroundings Georgia noticed a large pile of dark fluids on more pine needles. Moving closer to examine it, immediately she knew it was blood. It was a shade darker than what she had found yesterday and came to the conclusion because another night had passed. Grabbing the camera from her bag, Georgia quickly snapped a polaroid and waited for it to print. She knew that if she collected samples, she he would have to give them to the police crew. Placing the rubber gloves on and opening a small bag, Georgia grabbed the pine needles and closed the small bag.

Approaching the large rock, Georgia looked around. She had a feeling she was missing something and knew she was right as she walked around the rock and found a cabin. This was what Bruce was hiding! With her rubber gloves still on, Georgia walked to the door and began to open it. Immediately hit with the worst stench she had ever smelt in her life, she closed the door. Thankful she did not eat breakfast, Georgia searched her bag for something to cover her nose and mouth with. Making a small cover from a handkerchief she prepared herself.

Opening the door again, she used her flashlight to guide her. No matter how much she prepared herself, she would have never been prepared enough for what she saw. On the ground were several sharp utensils. Grabbing a knife from the ground, Georgia placed it in another small bag. A large pool of half dried blood sat near the wall. Whatever happened here was pure evil, there was too much blood for it to be an accident. Taking as many pictures as she could, Georgia was startled by the sound of branches breaking outside. Running out the front door, she hid in the trees keeping an eye out for who or whatever was out there.

Bruce was walking towards the cabin as the stench had reached him. He knew that something or someone had been inside, it never smelt like this before. Bruce was also sure to clean up before the searches began. Shaking his head Bruce grabbed a small mask from his pocket. Opening the front door to the cabin, he did not remember there being this much blood when he left several days before. Georgia walked as Bruce nonchalantly walked around the cabin, pulling the camera up, she took several pictures of Bruce.

Bruce grabbed the scalpel and scissors from the ground and placed them in the sink. Looking around Bruce noticed the knife was missing. The knife he used to stab Stacy in the leg and create various cuts along her skin. The knife he used to kill her as he listened to her last breath. Standing in the middle of the kitchen, he could not remember if he had buried the knife with Stacy.

Georgia watched as Bruce disappeared down the hallway, moving cautiously away from the trees. Georgia continued around the large rock and up another hill. Bruce must have come to the cabin a different way, or else he would have seen the bike Georgia placed on the tree. There were large piles of what looked like misplaced dirt in several areas. The further she got the more it had looked misplaced.

Georgia continued to check behind her, making sure that Bruce was not following her. Knowing that he had something to hide, she now knew what it was. The only problem was, Georgia had no idea how she would get Bruce to confess. Needing to return to the Bernet's cabin before anyone got too worried, Georgia reached Mrs. Bernet's bike and began pedaling as fast as she could. If Bruce saw her, there would be no telling what he would do. All she knew is she needed a plan.

Chapter Twenty Five

Georgia sat in her room in the Bernet's cabin and began thinking of a plan. Something that no one would know. She pondered the idea of asking Detective Raven for help or if she should do it all on her own. The decisions came crashing over her like the waterfall Stacy had brought her to.

Detective Raven showed up to the cabin in the early evening. Georgia greeted him at the door and welcomed him in.

"Good evening, we got the results back from the lab and I did not want to have this conversation over the phone. Please sit down Mr. Bernet."

Grabbing the hand of his wife, Mr. Bernet listened to the direction of detective Raven.

" Using the samples that both of you have provided, the lab compared them to the blood on the pine needles found yesterday. It was a match, meaning that the blood we have found on our searches indeed belongs to Stacy."

The sobs of Mrs. Bernet permeated the quiet air. The moment that everyone had been dreading was upon them

"I know this is not the news you were hoping to hear, but we don't have any evidence that she is deceased at this time either. The blood could be from an open wound and Stacy might not have been able to find her way back here. With that being said, we are going to continue the search tomorrow morning. As always you are welcome to join us but you can decide not to. Please keep in mind as of right now we are searching for a wounded but alive Stacy. If the search comes up without more evidence, our

chief will shut down the searches. I hope that whatever tomorrow brings will give you all and us a better understanding ."

Everyone agreed that they would continue on the search the following morning, but before detective Raven could leave. Georgia asked which area they would be looking. Detective Raven let them know they would follow an area that was further than where they found the blood the day before. That gave Georgia the answer she needed to continue her investigation of Bruce. The cabin Bruce did not want anyone to find was now safe from everyone but Georgia.

There were several ideas that floated through Georgia's mind. Should she just confront Bruce right away? Should she hang out with him like Stacy did? There were many things, but she decided on one. One that brought as much surprise to Georgia as it would Bruce. Georgia would get all the tools she needed and wait for Bruce at the cabin.

Knowing that the Bock's would be joining in today's search, Georgia minded each move Bruce made. The closer someone stepped towards one of those mysterious piles of dirt, the more nervous he looked. Making the connection that something or someone was buried under these piles, make Georgia weary of her plan. Something horrible happened in that cabin and she wanted to get the details down. From the view he got yesterday there were not many places inside the cabin to hide. The only area Georgia didn't go was down the hallway. From what she saw in the kitchen and what she assumed to be the living room. The only place to sit was a couple of old stools, not a very homey place.

Bruce patrolled the move of each person out on the search, including the police crew. Detective Raven informed them earlier that the helicopter was not able to pick anything up with the amount of tree coverage. Bruce had to do everything in his power to make sure no one would be going backwards. If they did, they were sure to find the cabin. The areas where he had buried the women and their belongings are scattered throughout this area. If there was any suspicion that someone had dug the ground up, Detective Raven would be sure to get some shovels out here. Bruce needed to prevent that at all costs less they discover his victims

There would be two spots that were freshly dug, one where Stacy's belongings were and the other where her decomposing body is. As the search party got closer to that area, Bruce attempted to veer everyone away. To his dismay, he was unsuccessful. Georgia noticed Bruce's reaction to this area, and the fact he was trying to drive everyone away.

"Detective Raven? Would you mind if we searched the area over there?" Georgia called from behind the Bock family.

As soon as the words left her lips, Bruce flung around. With a straight face, Georgia stared at the coldness laid across Bruce's face. She had never seen his eyes look that cold, dark and staring at what felt like into her soul. Georgia knew there had to be something over there. Could it be Stacy? Detective Raven and his police crew switched directions, only walking a couple hundred feet before they came across dirt that looked like it had recently been disturbed.

"Send someone to get shovels. We are going to need to see if there is anything here or if an animal may have done it ." Detective Raven let go of one of the police man's shoulders.

After what had felt like an eternity waiting for them to return, Two of the policemen arrived back at the spot with three shovels. Detective Raven grabbed one and began to dig. Georgia, who was sitting on a rock nearby, got up. Bruce intently watched as the dirt he moved a week ago was being dug up again. This had never happened before. The only thing that had dug up the bodies of his victims was a bear right before hibernation.

Bruce could feel tightness in his throat, he needed to chill out or someone would notice his behavior had changed. Detective Raven bent down holding up a small piece of clothing. He pulled the clothing father out of the ground and a shirt appeared. Stacy's shirt. Covered in blood and dirt, what Georgia thought had become a nightmare was indeed real. Stacy had been murdered. Rushing to Mr. Bernet's side, Georgia tried to hold him up as his body sank into the ground, hitting his knees.

"I need everyone to return to the cabin, this investigation has now become a homicide." Detective Raven stood tall, his words so clear and kept repeating in Georgia's mind.

Some of the police crew escorted everyone back to the Bernet's cabin. Detective Raven stayed back to wait for the chief of police to show up. Bruce was furious, Georgia opened her mouth. She knew something or at least she thought she did. Bruce wanted to know how. How did she know there was something in that area, why not anywhere else but there?

"Georgia, we need to talk." Bruce did not care who was watching, instead he needed to know everything Georgia knew.

"I will not be going anywhere, in case you haven't read the room, we just found out my best friend was murdered, their daughter." With a firm tone, Georgia hoped Bruce got the message. Georgia understood that her plan needed to have a safety net, something to protect herself from whom she now considered a monster.

Detective Raven quickly walks through the front door, followed closely by the chief of police. He had only shown his face once, and that was before this case became a homicide. Everything they knew about him was carried on from Detective Raven and the policemen.

The chief scanned the room, his eyes stopping on Mr and Mrs Bernet.

"I am sorry for your loss, we will do everything in our power to find out what happened to your daughter and who is responsible. I know that at the beginning of this case there were interviews already conducted. Since you all have continued to be the ones out searching for Stacy, I would like to reinterview you all. There is no harm in doing this, I understand the frustration that can come and of course each of you have rights. If you don't mind, I would like to start with the parents of Stacy Bernet."
The chief's words seemed to do very little in offering any condolences. He had a job to do and came to accomplish what he could.

By the time Mr. Bock had finished his interviews, it was almost midnight. Each of the parents had given their permission to have their children interviewed,

Bruce was the only one closest to eighteen. The chief

and Detective Raven were at the kitchen table as Georgia

sat down. She told them the same statement from the

first time Detective Raven interviewed her. The new

information she had and the cabin she saw, Georgia

withheld. They were police, if they were conducting

their search well enough they would have stumbled upon

it on their own.

Bruce watched intensely as Georgia sat across

from the chief giving her statement again. He wondered

what she was telling them. Did she mention the cabin?

Did she even know about the cabin? Was it just pure

coincidence that she led them to find Stacy's belongings?

Bruce sat on the couch until it was his turn to give a

statement. He did not mention seeing Stacy after they

went to the cabin she was restoring. He said they returned home and had dinner at the Bernet's cabin. After that all he knew was that she had gone missing and had been helping search for her.

Reviewing each statement, the chief and Detective Raven stood up. Thanking everyone for their cooperation.

"I know this has and will continue to be hard on all of you. Please know that you can join us tomorrow for a final search then the police department will completely take over. Mr and Mrs Bernet, we will keep you informed of any findings. Thank you for your hospitality, I hope to see you all in the morning." Detective Raven motioned for his crew to follow the chief out the door.

Glancing at the clock Georgia knew there would be little sleeping going on in this cabin. It was already four A.M and Georgia knew it would not be long until the police crew was back. Georgia thought Bruce was going to ask her to come talk again, instead he walked out the front door with his family.

Chapter Twenty Six

Without any sleep Georgia and Mr. Bernet is out the door to participate in the final search they get to be involved with. Georgia's heart was heavy but she knew that Stacy's parents and sister's were much heavier.

" Georgia? " Mr. Bernet stops and turns towards her. *" Thank you for being here. You were the best friend to Stacy and you have always been welcome in our home. Please know that no matter what happens today, you will forever be allowed over. "* Georgia could hear the emotion in Mr. Bernet's voice. He sounded as if he was attempting to choke back tears.

"I will do all I can in order to bring justice for Stacy. " Georgia grabs Mr. Bernet's hand and gives it a squeeze. She loved this family as much as she did her own, there

was no way that she would let anyone get away with this.

When Georgia and Mr. Bernet arrived at the area they were all escorted away from the day before, there were already policemen digging. In every direction she turned, someone was ripping a shovel through the earth. The Bock family stood next to them. They each looked around in shock, even Bruce. Georgia could not figure out why he would be shocked.

For a couple hours, each of them searched around the area where the police were digging. Georgia kept a close eye on Bruce as he was being watchful to every area that was being dug up. The swelling in Bruce's throat never went away. Instead with each swallow it seemed to get bigger. Touching around his neck, there were no swollen glands. He must have been imagining it.

One of the policemen was digging a hole next to where Bruce had laid Stacy's body. A couple more inches of dirt and the policemen might be able to see the tarp Bruce wrapped her lifeless body in. Bruce could not fathom how he would react, but before he could figure it out, Stacy's body was being pulled out of the ground.

Georgia stood there paralyzed as a body was being placed on the ground. *Please don't be Stacy* rang through her mind. As detective Raven began to unravel the tarp, the horrible stench that reminded her of the smell from that cabin came rushing through Georgia's nose. It was Stacy. Mr. Bernet rushed over to look at his daughter. Tears rolled down his face as he screamed Stacy's name holding her lifeless body. Georgia's eyes met Bruce's, that same coldness filled his eyes was still there accompanied with a smirk on the corner of his mouth. The confession Georgia wanted showed right before her.

No words were spoken between leaving Stacy's body with the coroner, and the trip back to Bernet's cabin. Georgia stayed with Mr. Bernet until the police made them leave. The chief of police was already at the house informing Georgia's parents and Mrs. Bernet about their discovery. Georgia heard the unbearable cries from outside, she was not ready to go in. She needed to focus on what she was going to do about Bruce. He had proven he was dangerous, which meant Georgia had to be dangerous as well. She knew that Mr. Bernet kept a gun on the table beside his bed. There were a couple issues with that, Georgia had never fired a gun before and she was not sure how to get the gun without anyone seeing.

Georgia was deep into thought when a blanket was slung over her shoulder. Her father sat down next to her and everything she was thinking disappeared as she bawled.

Chapter Twenty Seven

Georgia waited for the right time to say something to Bruce. Deep down she knew he was the one who murdered Stacy. Everything about him made it stick out even more to Georgia. She wondered if others had noticed his behavior and the way he smirked when detective Raven unraveled Stacy's body from the tarp. It was only three in the morning, Georgia was unable to sleep with revenge of her best friend on her mind. She needed to talk to Sam, he would help her understand things in a clearer mindset.

Not minding the time at all, Georgia knocked on the door to Sam's cabin. To her surprise, Sam was already up and making coffee. *Old people get up way too early. Georgia* couldn't help but think to herself. Sam opened the door and before a word was spoken between the two, he pulled Georgia in his skinny arms.

"Everything is going to be okay, justice will make its way to you and the Bernet family." Sam's words seemed to bring comfort to Georgia, but without thinking the words she spoke back startled Sam.

"I know who did it."

Pulling away from the hug, Sam stepped over to the kitchen pulling down two cups. Pouring the coffee, Georgia wondered if he heard her.

"Sam?"

"Are you sure or do you just think you know? Grief can blind people, Georgia." Sam backed a few paces and looked at Georgia.

Placing the two cups of coffee at the table, Georgia and Sam sat down. She took a deep breath and braced herself to tell Sam everything she knew.

"Bruce Bock. During the last couple searches, where it was too dangerous for you to go he acted weird. There was an area where he pulled the police away from. I went to that area the next day and there was a cabin. It was hard to find at first, but now it had become clear as day. The smell protruding throughout the house was something I had never smelt before, not until they pulled Stacy's body from the ground Sam."

Grabbing the photos she took from her bag, Georgia placed them on the table for Sam to look at. His eyes began to water, Georgia knew he believed her.

"I sat in the tree's when I heard someone coming. It was Bruce, he walked into that cabin as if he had been there

before. As if he knew what went on. The amount of blood and the wounds on Stacy would fall hand in hand. I know it's Bruce. " Georgia took a sip of her coffee, waiting for Sam to speak.

"The sad thing is, Georgia, I think you are right. When those other women went missing, Bruce was staying at his family's cabin. He would disappear for long periods of time, at various hours of the day. I have spent some time watching him and when I went to warn Stacy that night, Bruce watched me walk back to my cabin. What are you going to do?

Georgia took a deep breath. She had spent so much time asking herself the same question and she could only find one answer.

"I am going to kill him."

Sam showed no emotion, he knew that was the right thing to do. Justice for all the other women and Stacy.

"Be careful, your secret will always be safe with me."

The two of them sat in silence until the coffee was gone. Georgia knew what she had to do and there was no time to be wasted. Georgia stood up from the table, nodded at Sam. walking out the front door of his cabin, Georgia headed to the cabin in the woods.

As the police were doing their own investigation, Bruce was steering clear of the Bernet's cabin. Since the last search and the finding of Stacy's dead body he had only been over there twice. He knew that in a situation like this people would keep their distance from a grieving family. He also knew that if he kept away for too long it would start to look suspicious. The cabin in the woods needed to be cleaned still, Bruce had to get out any evidence that Stacy was ever in there.

Packing a few cleaning supplies and a bucket, Bruce headed up the mountain. The sun was still tucked away, as the day had not fully started. Watching closely to make sure there was no one following him, Bruce reached the path to the cabin. Still no one but the deceased that knew about this cabin, or at least that Bruce was aware of. The policemen had not returned this morning to finish looking in the area where Bruce buried Stacy. That gave him roughly enough time to clean up the cabin and get back to his family's cabin before anyone saw him.

Opening the door to the cabin Bruce walked in closing the door behind him. Placing the supplies he brought with him, he stood there looking for the place to start. Kneeling down, he picked a rag up and moved towards the pile of blood on the ground. A sound of someone clearing their throat startled him and he whipped around.

Georgia was sitting on the stool that Bruce placed a tied up Stacy to.

"Coming to clean your mess before the police get here?"

With no questioning in her throat, Bruce placed the rag in the bucket looking at Georgia.

"How did you know this was here? Why are you here?"

Without a spill of warmth in her voice, Georgia walked over to the counter in the kitchen.

"I know you killed Stacy."

Turning around, Bruce was now standing. He could not believe the words that just came from

Georgia's mouth. How did she know? He was so careful, just like he had been with all the women before *"If you didn't open your mouth, no one would have ever found Stacy. Just like the other women. Lost souls that a bear possibly ate. She was a fighter though. Stacy would not give up. She even tried to run away but something about being stabbed in the thigh kind of prevented that."* A small chuckle formed from Bruce. Georgia wanted to hear what he had to say. She stood in silence, peering at Bruce from across the room.

"Let me take a couple guesses, here. You want to know why, how, when it all happened? Well Georgia, while you were off with my brother, Stacy was left alone. She became the perfect victim, other than having a snotty friend like you. She was always alone in the woods. I scared her a couple times, but still out of pure stupidity

she kept going back to that cabin. She got what was

coming." Bruce did not hold back the belly laugh as his

last words came out.

Out of everything Georgia could have felt

hearing those words, she felt anger. She would not cry in

front of this monster. That would give him too much

satisfaction, instead she pushed herself off the counter

and walked over to Bruce.

"You have some nerve to think she wouldn't be found."

Georgia knew that in her bag, placed next to the

stool was Mr. Bennet's gun. Yes, she did not know how

to use it, but it couldn't be that hard. She had watched

several movies and Stacy always talked about the hunts

Mr. Bernet went on. The only thing now was for Bruce

to continue talking until Georgia decided it was time.

Bruce walked over to the drawer where he kept the knife's.

"You are a very stupid girl for coming here. What were you hoping to find?"

Grabbing a small knife, Bruce knew that Georgia might not have the fight that Stacy did. Georgia watched as Bruce turned around holding a knife.

"Bruce, you underestimate me. You don't know me, and quite frankly I am not sure I do either. What you have done to those women and their families. You are a monster. The police might not see through the lies you fed them, but I do"

Bruce just looked at Georgia and once again began to laugh.

"And you are going to save the world now? You have nothing, no proof. Are you going to turn me into the police on assumptions?"

Georgia was now laughing.

"You don't know what proof I have, but no. I will not be tuning you into the police. We both know what you have done."

Bruce lunges towards Georgia, the blade of the knife in his hands skids across her arm as she pulls it up in defense. Georgia can barely feel the pain, as her blood drops on the floor. Reaching into her bag, she feels the handle of the gun. Bruce looks at her, wondering what she was hiding.

Without shaky hands, Georgia points the gun at Bruce.

"Looks like you are the stupid one now."

Bruce backed away from Georgia. He knew that a knife never won in a gunfight.

"What do you want to know?" Bruce's voice showed emotion for the first time.

"I do not want to know anything, if you choose to talk that will be on you. You haven't kept quiet the whole time I've been here so why stop?"

Georgia takes a seat on the stool. Keeping the gun faced towards Bruce, she waits.

"You know my brother would never be with the person that killed his brother. You two have been inseparable, you want to ruin that?"

Georgia shakes her head.

"You see, what happens between Jonah and I will be none of your business Bruce. You have had zero

persuasion on our friendship all summer. The only thing

you cared about was you."

Looking around Bruce can see that the sun is starting to come up. Both him and Georgia knew that the police would soon be in the woods no farther than a mile away soon. Georgia turns her attention back on Bruce, who has become antsy. Georgia felt good having the upper hand.

"I killed all those women and Stacy because it brings me joy. It started last year and since then it just comes naturally. The feeling of taking someone's last breath had become an obsession. There is only one way to explain it, Stacy tried. She knew that you all would go looking for her. I had high hopes that she would never be found. There must have been something different about

the police crew, they have never looked for someone this

long. That's what made it easy."

Bruce knew if he tried to attack Georgia, it wouldn't work. Not with her sitting there pointing a gun at him. Instead he continued to tell her the things about Stacy's last breath and how much she tried to hold on. Georgia listened to each detail Bruce told her. She couldn't imagine the pain that her best friend was going through. How afraid she must have been. She was so innocent, only trying to restore that cabin, wanting it to be her future home. Now she would never be able to do any of that. Instead her life was taken by the hands of evil.

When Bruce finished talking, Georgia stood up. Grabbing her bag she walked towards the door. Holding up the gun, Georgia steadied herself. As she turned

around

"You will never get to hurt another woman."

Boom.

The sound of the gun firing ricocheted off the

walls of the cabin. Bruce's body snapped in half as he

fell to the ground. Georgia continued outside and closed

the door. She was now a killer, but she knew it was for

Stacy.

www.ingramcontent.com/pod-product-compliance
Lightning Source LLC
Chambersburg PA
CBHW030534030726
47495CB00004B/982